The Mystery of the

WAGNER
WHACKER

The Mystery of the
WAGNER
WHACKER

Joseph Romain

WARWICK
YA!
SPORTS

Note about U.S. Edition: The author takes great pleasure in introducing the Mystery of the Wagner Whacker to American readers. Readers familiar with the Canadian edition will note some minor changes in language, reflecting the differences between Canadian and American colloquial use.

ISBN 1-895629-94-2

Published by Warwick Publishing Inc.
388 King Street, West, Suite 111, Toronto, Ontario M5V 1K2
1424 North Highland Avenue, Los Angeles, CA 90027

Distributed by Firefly Books Ltd.
3680 Victoria Park Avenue, Willowdale, Ontario M2H 3K1

Design: Kimberley Young, mercer digital design

Printed and bound in Canada

This book is dedicated to Gail, Breeze,
Lionel and Simone Rose.

Some other books by Joseph Romain:

The West Windsor Nine. Vanwell Press, 1997.

The Wagner Whacker. Vanwell Press, 1996.

Two Minutes for Roughing. Lorimer, 1994.

Ladies' Day: A Woman's Guide to Pro Baseball. Warwick Publishing, 1997.

Legends of Hockey, Publications International. 1995 (Consulting Editor).

20th Century Chronicles of Ice Hockey, Publications International. 1994
(Cons. Ed.).

Wayne Gretzky: Simply the Greatest. Brompton Books, 1992, 1994.

The Athletics: A Baseball Dynasty. Gallery Books, 1991.

Hockey Superstars. Brompton Books, 1991, 1992, 1994.

Images of Glory: The Toronto Maple Leafs. McGraw-Hill Ryerson, 1990.

Toronto. Whitecap Books, 1990, 1992, 1994.

The Stanley Cup. Bison Books, 1990, 1992, 1994.

Hockey Hall of Fame: The Official History of the Game and Its Greatest Stars.
Doubleday, 1988.

The Pictorial History of Hockey. Gallery Books, 1987, 1990, 1994, 1996.

About the Author:

Joseph Romain grew up in Windsor, Ontario in a big house with more brothers and sisters than he can count. He now lives in Toronto, in a big house, and is the father of more kids than he can count. Joseph writes full time and works part time in a large metropolitan library, where he answers questions and helps kids with science projects and language skills. He worked for many years as a librarian and curator at the NHL's Hockey Hall of Fame and Museum, and has written many books about the history of ice hockey. He has also worked on trail crews in Glacier Park, on high rise buildings as a glazier in Toronto, and as a ghost-buster in small towns in Ontario. *The Wagner Whacker* was judged the first runner up for the Canadian Children's Book Of The Year for 1997, and his previous novel, *Two Minutes For Roughing*, was a Choice selection of the Canadian Children's Book Centre. His third novel, *The West Windsor Nine* will appear in the fall of 1997. He is currently working on a novel which takes place in "Little India" in Toronto, and on a picture book about his father's immigration from Beirut to Detroit in the 1920's.

1

Who's Moving What?

Matt Killburn jerked the front door open. A tall dark boy stood on the verandah frantically smacking a baseball into his mitt.

"Yeah, what d'ya want, Salaam?" Matt snarled.

"Are you coming, Killburn?" Sanji sputtered impatiently, spinning around to face him. "It's the third inning already. Hereford's behind the plate and they're killing us!" Matt suddenly remembered the Sunday morning exhibition game. They'd planned it for nine- thirty, and it was already after ten o'clock.

It wasn't like him to forget about baseball. In fact, forgetting a game was so unusual, it scared him a little. Especially this year.

This was their year. Matt and Sanji were finally moving up into more challenging territory; they'd be rookies in the Waterloo-Kitchener Major Pee Wee Baseball League. Every team needs good pitchers, so Sanji was assured a place on the team, and The Wings needed solid catching more than they needed hitting, so in spite of his less than spectacular .196 average for Minor Pee Wee, Matt got a starting spot in the lineup.

A spot in the lineup that he wouldn't be able to fill. It made him sick. All those years of hard work, and now, when they could really prove something — playing with serious ball players, up to fifteen years old — he had to quit.

So he didn't feel much like playing baseball today. He blinked at Sanji through the screen door. "I forgot about the game," Matt mumbled. "It's only an exhibition. I'll be there later maybe."

Sanji squinted at him. He flipped his long black hair back over his head and twisted his cap into place. "What are you talking about?" he snorted, in his crisp British voice, "Are you sick or what? Yesterday you couldn't play because your mom wanted to take a drive in the country, and today you'll be there later maybe? You know what I think; I think you're sick in the head, mate. You oughtta see a doctor..." He tapped his head and rolled his eyes.

Matt gazed across the road to the park, his stomach churning. He used to play there with his dad, before his dad got the cancer. He remembered this same churning deep in his stomach from two years ago, when he saw the little letter board outside the funeral room with his dad's name on it. "Albert Killburn" it said in white letters on the black board.

He remembered his Uncle Costa taking him out to the funeral parlor porch for some cold, fresh air. Costa thought cold air was the cure for anything.

"I know what you're going through, Matt." Costa put his pudgy hand on Matt's shoulder. "It hurts kinda like when you're hungry, eh? Only worse. Way down in your guts. But it'll get better. You'll see." Then he looked down, and his face sort of changed. He knelt down so they were on the same eye level, and Matt knew he was giving it to him straight.

"Look, it won't stop hurting. It'll always hurt this much. Only, after a while it hurts less and less often." Costa was crying. Not big, slurpy crying, but buttery eyes and sweaty hands sort of crying.

"At first," he said, "you'll notice the times when it doesn't hurt, when it's not the only thing you're thinking about. It'll surprise you that you're laughing, or that you haven't thought about him today. Then, in time, it only hurts once in a while. It'll hurt just the same as it does now, only, it's not as often. That's the way it is for me, anyway..."

It helped. Matt had felt a little better. And it was true. As the years went by he did laugh, and run and not think about his dad.

But when he did, he always got that same sick feeling. That's the way he felt now. Empty, sick, and afraid.

Matt stood looking out at Sanji's small dark face grinning in through the screen door, and he thought he was going to throw up. Matt slammed the heavy door hard on its hinges. He lumbered up the stairs to his room, slamming that door too.

"Matt? Is that Sanji?" his mother called from the kitchen. He was sick and mad at her, and he didn't want to answer. "Matt? Are you going out with Sanji?" she called from the bottom of the stairs. He ignored her.

"Clack, clack, clack!" The knocker smacked on the small brass door plate. "Hey, Killburn," Sanji hollered, "Killburn, what are you doing? Come on, open the door!" Matt's mother opened the door, with a worried smile on her face.

"He's sick Mrs. Zonjic. He says he doesn't want to play ball. Last time he didn't want to play he had to get his tonsils out! Maybe you better call the doctor, Mrs. Zee. Maybe they grew back..."

Matt had his father's last name, Killburn, but his mother's name was Mrs. Zonjic. Sanji just called her "Mrs. Zee."

"His tonsils are fine," she groaned, "It's not his tonsils I'm worried about."

"Come on, Killburn," Sanji called from the front hall, "are you coming or not?"

"Matt's had a bit of news, Sanji. I think he should be the one to tell you about it. Why don't you go up to his room?"

Sanji closed the screen door and pulled off his sneakers. He dropped them onto the boot tray, and followed Maria into the kitchen. Mrs. Zonjic was usually up for anything. She was his friend's mother, but to Sanji, she was more like a big sister. She told jokes, she listened to rock music, and she could help with math. Today she looked more like a mother. She looked more like Sanji's own mother, who never joked or listened to rock music, and did not understand modern mathematics.

"I think you should talk to him, Sanji. I don't think you'll be too happy either, but maybe you can cheer him up a bit. Take the bag of Oreos up with you."

Sanji knew it had to be serious. Mrs. One Each was giving him the whole bag of Oreos to take up to Matt's No Food Allowed bedroom.

"Do you have any pop to wash them down, Mrs. Zee?" he tried, pushing his luck.

"Nice try, Sanji," she frowned. "Okay, I'll meet you halfway. What about juice?" She poured two glasses and handed them to him on a tray. He stuck the bag between his teeth, splayed his ball glove over his head and reached out for the tray.

"Try not to spill it, eh Sanji," she said, watching him bob and weave through the doorway, keeping glove, bag and tray all balance and sway to the rhythm of the stairs.

Sanji flipped the handle with a free thumb and pushed the bedroom door open with his foot. "Yo, Maestro Matthew, what is going on around here?" he grinned, "I didn't even have to raid the kitchen! Mrs. Clean just gave me juice and a bag of Oreos to go! What's the scoop? I gotta get back to the game."

Matt didn't look up. He was lying on his stomach with a Mad magazine spread out on the bed in front of him.

"We're moving." Matt turned his head so that Sanji couldn't see his face.

"What d'ya mean?" Sanji popped a cookie into his mouth and raised an eyebrow. "Who's moving what?" He figured that maybe he'd heard wrong. Then he wondered if Matt was crying. He remembered what Matt's mother had said in the kitchen.

"You mean, moving ? Like you're going to move? No way!" Sanji's first worry was for the team. Who's going to replace Matt Killburn as catcher? But before he said it he stopped himself. Matt was definitely crying. And it was catchy.

"Where are you going?" Sanji forgot about the ball game he had left in the third inning. This was more important than winning or losing a baseball game. "When are you supposed to move?" he said, choking on the words.

"Do you have to go to a new school?" He could feel his eyes start to sting. If he talked any more, he knew that he'd start blubbering. His stomach felt squishy, and his throat was tightening up.

"My mom's going to work from home, and she bought a farm.

In Fergus!" Matt was crying hard now, wiping his eyes with his sleeve and keeping his face turned in to the magazine. "They planned the whole thing... Costa and her... We're going in June," he sobbed.

June! thought Sanji. The season is just starting in June! Matt couldn't even be on the team! Nobody else could even catch his fastball, and nobody else knew how to ask for the pitches. Most catchers just caught the balls the hitters missed. With Matt Killburn behind the plate, they were up against a master of the game!

Sanji knew who was responsible for half the batters he struck out. More than half. Matt knew when to call for a change-up, when to signal for strikes, when to pitch around a hot batter, when to go for the pick-off at second base. Nobody could replace his rhythm behind the plate. But this wasn't just a catcher he was losing; this was Matt Killburn! His best friend. Moving.

He'd been the first one to make friends when Sanji came from India, and the only friend he ever thought he'd need. This was more serious than losing the best baseball player in the world, this meant his best friend — his brother, almost — was going away, and Sanji couldn't hold back any more. He sat on the floor, slurping up tears.

Matt crumpled the magazine and turned on his side, facing the wall. "Yesterday, when we went to the country, they stopped at a farm with a For Sale sign up. First they told me they were thinking about buying a house together, then they told me that we were moving to this farm. It's a few miles from Costa's store." He wasn't crying so much now, but Sanji could tell from the way he kept clearing his throat that he was going to start up again, any minute.

"So is your uncle going to live there too?" Sanji asked. Matt's uncle Costa was a cool guy. It wouldn't be as bad if he was going to live with them. At least there would be somebody to hang out with. And there was Costa's store, The Daily Mail and Trading Post. Costa lived upstairs from The Trading Post. It was a cross between a junk shop, a variety store, a coffee shop, and a souvenir stand. The Trading Post was very cool.

"No," Matt said, "Costa's not going to live with us, he's just buying it with my mom. They told me it was probably the only time that houses would be cheap enough for either of them to buy a place, and my mom can do her job from Fergus and drive into Kitchener for meetings and stuff." He punched the pillow under his head. "They didn't even ask me! They just figure I'm like furniture, like it doesn't matter if I don't want to move. Maybe I could live at your house, Sanj."

Sanji thought about what his mother would say to a permanent sleep over. "I don't think so... Have an Oreo." They sat in silence.

"June!" Sanji whistled, "That's less than a month from now!"

2

The Whacker

They heard the front door close and Costa hollered up the stairs. "Hey, Maria! Matt! Anybody home?" The two boys looked at each other and laughed at their red eyes. Sanji cocked his ear toward the door and Matt shrugged. Neither of them answered. Sanji took another cookie and pulled the ends off, scraping at the sweet middle with his front teeth. Costa was coming up the stairs. Sanji stuffed two more cookies into his cap and passed the bag over to Matt.

Costa was knocking gently on the door. "Hey, Matt, where's your mother?"

"I don't know," the boy mumbled.

"Can I come in?" he said from the hallway.

"It's not locked, Costa," Matt said flatly. He was mad at Costa too.

Matt's uncle came in and closed the door. "Hey, Sanji, how's it goin'? Matt tell you about the farm? Looks like a funeral in here." Nobody answered him. "I guess he told you.

"It's not that bad, you know. Fergus is a great town. I've been there goin' on three years. There's loads of kids, lots to do, they've got a really good hockey team... Once you guys get used to the idea, you're gonna like it there. Maria will expect you to come out and stay over, Sanji. It won't be bad, really. Hey, it's less than an hour away!"

"Costa?" Maria called from the bottom of the stairs. "Is that you?"

"No, it's the tooth fairy. I'm up here with Matt and Sanji." He turned to Sanji, "Gimme an Oreo, creep, or I'll tell her you guys've got the whole bag up here."

"That's extortion, Costa. Besides, she gave it to us," Sanji replied, tossing a cookie up to the grinning grownup. Costa's face looked fatter and rounder because of the shape of his mustache. It was like a fat black caterpillar had crawled in and made camp over his lip.

"She gave you guys a bag of cookies to eat in Matt's room? Wow, talk about a guilty conscience." He wagged his head and opened the door, leaving the two boys alone in the room. He descended the stairs and gave his sister a hug and a peck on the cheek. The move from Kitchener to Fergus would be a problem for Matt, but Costa felt it was the best thing for the family.

"Maria, listen," he grinned. "I've got a couple things that might shake him out of his funk. I picked up a very cool, very old baseball bat for him, and I've managed to get three seats at the Skydome for today's game. Seventeen rows up behind the first base bag. You two want to go?"

"Costa, that's great! Why don't you take the boys? I think Matt and Sanji probably could use the time together. It gives me a chance to get some stuff done around here, too."

"Check, Sis. You're probably right. How's he taking it?"

"Not as well as I figured he would. I feel awful. He hasn't said three words to me since we got home last night. If he's trying to make me feel guilty he's doing a great job. I'm not sure this was such a great idea." She opened the fridge and started making sandwiches for the road. "What time is the game?"

"It's a one-thirty-five start, so if we want to get there for batting practice, we'd better go now. D'ya think they'll want to see the Twins' batting practice?"

"Why don't you ask them?" she said, smearing yellow margarine on the bread.

Costa trudged back up the stairs and knocked on the door. "You guys want to see Dave Winfield in a Minnesota jersey? I got seats so close we can shake his hand."

Matt had his magazine spread out again, and Sanji was working on the second row of cookies. Matt didn't look up from the magazine. "I don't know," he said.

"I do. We're going," said Sanji, draining his glass of juice. "Come on Matt, this is Dave Winfield for Pete's sake. Scott Erickson's starting today, right?"

"You got it Sanji, we get to see the Minnesota wonder boy work," Costa said, tapping the back of Matt's head with the tickets. "Call your mom, Sanj, I'll get this guy ready to roll. Come on, Matthew, the hot dogs are on me."

Nobody mentioned Fergus, farms or moving day all the way to Toronto. The drive from Kitchener to the Skydome took about an hour and a half, and they talked about the new-look Blue Jays, the latest developments in the Kelly Gruber saga, and the look of this year's Upper Deck baseball card set.

Costa knew a bit about baseball cards. Not as much as Matt or Sanji, but he had set up a display case full of cards in his variety store in Fergus, and he had to know enough to keep up with the local kids, so Matt and Sanji had taught him the basics a couple of years ago. Costa had been pretty valuable to them, too.

Every year, Matt and Sanji made up their own teams with cards, picking players from all the American League rosters, and played a dream season by taking each player's weekly stats, and recording them as wins or losses for their imaginary squads. They were able to get all the obscure cards they needed from Costa, and he was able to sell most of the cards they didn't want. Costa was cool.

Usually, when Matt came to the Skydome with Costa, they went in through Gate Two, pathway to the lowly upper decks, the nosebleed seats. Today they headed for Gate Eleven, field level heaven.

They passed under the huge bronze sculptures set into the wall high above the sidewalk. Matt looked up at the group of gigantic baseball fans cheering at a ball game. One of them had his thumb to his nose, fingers extended, giving a raspberry to the ump. That was how Matt felt. Like he was thumbing his nose at the stream of people who were turning left to the cheap seats.

He felt pretty important handing his ticket to the woman at the gate. She ripped it and handed the stub to him with a smile. "Great day for a ball game," she said. "It's sunshine and batting practice inside."

The Jays played more like it was a batting clinic than a ball game. Their pitcher Jack Morris was brilliant, giving up only two runs, and the Blue Jays scored eleven times. The Jays weren't just good, they were a relentless attack squad with "Championship" written all over them. Last year's hero Dave Winfield was stone cold, getting no hits for three at bats.

Matt and Sanji weren't just fans, they were dedicated students of baseball. As far back as Matt could remember, life had begun in April with spring training and ended in October with the World Series. In the winter, he read books about baseball, and watched reruns of the playoffs and all-star games on video. And he played it every day.

He knew enough about the game to know that to make the Big Time, you had to be born with more than a love of the game and above average skills; the Big Time required the right type of body, and Matt was born with his mother's short legs, short arms and stubby fingers. Stubby was not exactly what big league scouts were looking for. And he wasn't exactly Dr. Longball when it came to hitting.

But he had an arm like a twelve-pound cannon and an understanding of the game which was far beyond his years. What he lacked as an athlete, he more than made up for with his knowledge of the finer points of baseball.

He had first met Sanji in grade three. Sanji had only been in grade two then, but 'the new kid' could snowball a pigeon off the school fence from thirty feet away! And he was left-handed! Matt decided, at that moment, that the new kid was destined for The Bigs. Long arms, long legs, long fingers. Deadly control. Raw talent.

Right then, Matt became a catcher. It was the best way to teach the logic and skills of pitching. He called the pitches, set up a system of signals, and by grade five had groomed the new kid from a gangling southpaw with promise into the unrivaled hero of the sandlot.

Matt was tough on the new kid. When he flashed a signal, he would expect the right pitch in the right location. If Sanji hit the glove, Matt would catch it. If he missed the target, Matt would lean forward on his knees, wag his head, and jerk his thumb over his shoulder. "Go get it, Salaam. I'm the brains here, not the ball caddie! You wanna throw me garbage, you can chase it yourself!"

It didn't take Sanji long to figure it out. If he didn't throw the pitches he was asked for then he'd spend more time running across the park than pitching. He learned to throw the ball into the glove.

By the time Matt was in grade six, only the imaginary batters could hit Sanji Salaam consistently. The older boys in the neighborhood took turns striking out and shaking their heads at the tall black kid on the mound. At recess games, even the teachers couldn't make contact.

Sanji didn't just throw faster than anybody else, he threw them where the hitters couldn't get at them, or where they didn't expect them. Matt was a master of finding the hitter's weak spots, and Sanji knew it. To Sanji, a game with Matt behind the plate was just like practice; he just threw the ball into the glove.

After the game, Costa led them up a side street to a small eatery. It was a tradition with Costa, that after the game he always went for coffee at the Kit Kat to let the traffic thin out. Maria usually had a beer, Costa had coffee, and Matt had a pistachio milkshake. The owner of the Kit Kat was a chubby Italian man named Al. Pictures of grinning Al with famous actors and actresses covered the walls.

Al was on the telephone behind a wide glass case full of cakes and fancy Italian pastries. He raised his eyebrows at Costa, smiling, and waved them to a table near the dessert counter. When he put down the phone he came over to their table and laid his cool, fat palm on Matt's head.

"Hello, Matthew. Good game, eh? Pistachio milk- shake, Kit Kat Koffee for the Big Fellow, and" Al turned to Sanji and smiled his big hearty smile, "what will you have, my young friend? Pistachio?"

"I've never had a pistachio milkshake," Sanji grinned up at Al, "Are they good?"

"Good?" Al said, cocking his head like he didn't quite understand. "Good? When my wife Cathy makes a pistachio milkshake, the angels sail down from heaven and whip the cream with the beating of their gossamer wings, my friend."

"It's true," Costa grunted, "I've seen them! Little angels, beating their... Come on, Al, he'll have a pistachio milkshake for cryin' out loud."

Sanji nodded agreement, and Al slipped behind the counter to give Cathy their order. Matt watched Al and Cathy elbowing each other behind the counter, and laughing at some joke. He slid over to the coffee bar and took a seat on the high stool.

"Well?" Al raised his thick eyebrow.

"Nothin'." Matt looked at Cathy. "I'm just watchin'."

"What's buggin' you Matt? It's all over your face like an outbreak of adolescent acne." Al puffed off some steam from the cappuccino coffee machine. "So Winfield didn't do nothin'. No big deal. Wait 'til you see what Paul Molitor is gonna do for the squad."

Matt looked at Al and shifted in his seat. "Costa and Maria bought a farm. We're gonna live there."

"Oh." Al tossed a tea towel over his shoulder and leaned his elbow on the coffee bar. "So. You're movin', eh? That's a tough one." He fixed Matt's eyes with his, just for a second, and said, "Yeah, that's a good reason for a long face."

"I can't believe they're making me move." Matt felt like he could confide in Al. He didn't know Al that well, but he had a soft, understanding face. He and Costa had been best friends when they were kids.

"Well, my friend, life is strange. Things change. Sometimes you can control things, and sometimes you can't." He looked up at the ceiling. "That's one thing that never changes. You're goin' through your life, havin' a good time, and suddenly, everything changes." He passed a flat hand across his eyes and exploded it over the counter, "Pshew! And all of a sudden, everything's different. It keeps happening all your life..."

Al picked up a black mug with red peppers on the side and wiped the rim with his tea towel. "But you know, when your life changes, when you move on, everything around you changes too." He blew some more steam out of the machine and set the mug under the spout.

"You know, when you move to a new place, Matt, all the mistakes you made in the past disappear. You get a new start; a clean slate, and you get to be whoever you want to be."

Al set the hot cup of milky coffee on a yellow saucer and headed over to the table, where Costa and Sanji were debating the possibility of a Blue Jays World Series win.

"Matt," Costa called over. "I've got something for you. You're gonna like it."

Whatever it was, Matt was determined not to like it. Costa was fumbling with the zipper of the big bag he'd brought. He pulled out a long, thin baseball bat and held it out to Matt. "It came in to the Trading Post last week. I gave Mr. Defranco thirty bucks' worth of lottery tickets for it." Matt hefted the bat, checking it for balance.

"Thirty bucks!" Matt sneered. "You gave him thirty bucks? Should have given him ten. Tops. Five at a yard sale," he said.

Actually, Matt thought the bat had a good feel. It was slim, but very dense. It seemed heavier than it should be. It probably wasn't as good as a Mizuno, or even a Slugger for that matter, but it was cool. But he wasn't going to let Costa know that. "As usual, Costa, you got taken."

"Let's have a look, then," Sanji said, taking the bat out of Matt's hands. "Smooth," he said, running his long fingers up the barrel. "Good weight. Heavy. Like a cricket bat." Sanji couldn't swipe the bat there in the coffee shop, but he held it up over his shoulder and hefted it. "I could hit with this bat."

Matt snickered over at Sanji. "You don't have to hit, Lefty. You just have to throw..."

Sanji cut him off, "...the ball into the glove. Yes, Master. I throw the ball into the glove." He sneered at Matt, "But a guy could hit with this thing.

"Hey, look here. It says 'Fergus'. It's made in Fergus! Check this out, Matt. It says THE WHACHER, Wacmor B something, something, something 'ment'. Equipment! It says Equipment!"

"Lemme see." Al sauntered over and took the bat from Sanji. He pulled glasses from his shirt pocket, and laid them on his nose. "It's THE WHACKER. Not 'Whacher'." He smiled at Sanji. "Uh huh. You're right. It's made in Fergus!" Al held on to the bat tightly, and laid it up against his forehead. "This bat's got something to say; it's got a story to tell... Matt, you should always look out for the improbable. This bat," he ran his fingers along the handle, "This is improbable... Listen to this bat."

"Yeah," Costa snorted, "it's gonna tell us about the angels beating the milkshakes. For cryin' out loud, Al, would you give us a break! If we wanted fruit cake, we'd have asked for it." He took the bat himself and shook it over his shoulder. "Feels like thirty bucks' worth to me."

Cathy came out from behind the counter with her hands on her hips. "If that bat's gonna tell stories, why don't you fellows all go off to the ballpark and listen to it, okay. I don't feel like cleaning up all the broken china!" She was smiling, but Costa put the bat back into his bag.

The conversation drifted back to baseball. Specifically, the look of the Blue Jays' new shortstop, Dick Schofield, and the prospects for a repeat of the World Series win. Now that was improbable!

3

The Loft

Matt slammed the back door of the Salaam's stationwagon. He pressed his face up against the window, flattening out his nose, and squishing his open lips into the glass. Mr. Salaam twirled his handlebar mustache and gave Matt and Costa a salute, smiling through his gold teeth. The white stationwagon crunched along Matt's new driveway, swung onto the pavement, and beeped a final goodbye.

Sanji and his father had brought the last load of stuff from the old house. Matt and Maria had been at the farm for nearly a week, and since school was over for the year, Sanji had been with them for most of it. Now, Sanji was going back to Kitchener for baseball practice with the Kitchener Wings. He would come back out to the farm with Maria tomorrow afternoon.

A few days ago Matt had conned Costa into paying the boys to inventory the store. They would write down the number and value of everything in the store, and figure out how much all his stuff was worth. What Matt really wanted was a box of this year's Upper Deck trading cards and a new pair of Nikes.

Costa had the cards, no problem, but he didn't exactly have a shoe department in the Trading Post. Matt had found a few boxes of canvas hi-top runners in the back room one day, but he didn't say anything about them. He could see his mother and Costa waving their arms around, telling him they always wore red canvas

23

hi-tops when they were his age.

There was no way he was going to make his first impressions around Fergus in a pair of red canvas hi-top runners. He decided that now was as good a time as any to bring up the subject of the money.

"Costa, you know how you agreed to give me and Sanji two boxes of cards and fifty bucks?"

"Yeah," Costa frowned. He suspected something was up right off.

"Well I wondered if you could sort of make it fifty bucks each. I mean, have you been back there? You've got stuff there that's been piled up since 1965! You should see some of the stuff behind the stock on the shelves. Did you know that you had headlights for Chevy trucks? A dozen of them. And inner tubes for ten speed bikes, I mean, who rides bikes with those skinny tires? What you need is a summer sale... A garage sale!"

He could see that Costa liked the idea. "Look, Sanji and I will be pulling all this stuff out anyway, and you can tell us how much the stuff costs, and we can put it on tables and benches on the street, and sell it cheap."

Costa was grinning. Matt knew he had him. "That's not a bad idea, Matt. Fifty bucks each to inventory the store and sell off all my goofups? It'll take you weeks to get that stuff sorted out you know."

Matt was on a roll, thinking fast. "Okay, so fifty bucks and ten percent." He thought he might as well go for the whole hog, adding, "each."

"Ten percent? Each? You're a crook, Matt."

"Come on, Costa, that stuff isn't worth anything sitting around in the back room. I'm offering you the opportunity of a lifetime! Two keen salesmen with a stake in the take."

"Okay, okay. All right. Fifty bucks each, and ten percent. To split. Not each."

Matt thought he might get fifteen percent out of him, but he knew how much stuff was piled up along the walls and shelves in the stock room. Ten percent was probably at least a hundred dollars, so he could count on a new pair of black sneakers.

"Okay. We'll start counting your stuff on Wednesday, and we'll have the sale when we're finished the inventory."

"Oh, sure," Costa laughed, "you mean the third Tuesday in February?"

"I mean this Saturday. Saturday is the day people expect to spend money. Don't you know anything about business?" Matt laughed when he said it, but he wondered how his uncle stayed in business. He didn't know anything about how to make money. He just cluttered up his store with so many things that people were bound to find something they needed if they looked long enough.

"I'll pick you guys up on Wednesday morning. Early. Like seven a.m. You know, Matt, I can't decide whether you're a crook or a genius. I've never seen you come out on the bad side of a deal. You're gonna be rich one day. So don't forget your Uncle Costa, eh?" He slid into his black pickup truck, and gunned it down the drive.

Matt was feeling pretty good about himself. He was beginning to like the idea of having the Trading Post so close to hand. Everybody in town knew Costa, and they all came in to buy papers and coffee, and to yak with him.

The only enemy Costa had was Costa. He gave away most of his profits in free second cups of coffee. Matt figured he knew a dozen things they could do to make some money at the store.

He had some boxes to unpack in his room, but he didn't feel much like it. His mother wouldn't be home for a while yet. He wandered into the barn and looked at the windows high above him. They were about fifty feet above the floor, and just below them a huge deck jutted out from the wall. On the opposite side of the barn, under the south windows, was another deck.

Matt noticed that the northern platform could be reached by a long ladder fastened to the wall. The south platform had no ladder, and seemed completely impossible to reach. He wondered how far he could see from the high windows. Probably for miles.

He gave the long ladder a shake, and decided that it was perfectly safe. The first dozen steps were no problem, but the higher he climbed, the more his body seemed to be drawn outward. He looked down once, decided that wasn't such a good idea, and fixed his eyes on each rung as he crept steadily upward.

He looked up to the platform just above him and stopped to rest, sweating and listening to his heart pounding in his ears. He grasped the next rung and felt it give. Every muscle in his body quivered into action. He grabbed for the lower rung and locked his fingers around it while he gathered up his nerve. Check the next one, he told himself, and reached up carefully. Finding the rung solid, he climbed on.

At the top of the ladder he found a trap door set into the platform. He reached up and shoved at it. It didn't budge. He could see that there was a bolt on the inside, and that it was locked.

Matt carefully examined the crack around the door. He could see where the latch came across, black against a stream of sunlight. The wood was worn around the edge, as though it had been sanded or rasped below the latch. He reached up and felt the rough wood, and his eye fell on the answer to the puzzle. There, above the ladder, was a small tool resting on a crossbeam. It was like a screwdriver with a sharp point. He took the screwdriver, and slid it along the crack. The latch swung back, and the door gave way!

Matt poked his head through the opening and glanced around at the room. Gingerly, he perched himself up onto the platform and swung his feet up and into the safety of the high loft. He slammed the trap door shut, loped across the wooden floor and plunked down on a very dusty sofa.

A sofa! How did anybody get a sofa up here? And all this other stuff! There was a table and chair, a chest of drawers, a bed, a bookshelf full of dusty old books, a washbasin, a stack of tin buckets, a trunk, and several oil lamps. Behind the bookshelf was a rocking chair facing the grimy windows. On the back of the chair were carved the initials 'A. W.' The platform was a lot bigger than he ever imagined from ground level. It was half the size of a gymnasium. And it looked like somebody lived up here!

There was a rail most of the way around the loft, and the floors were as solid as the earth, so he felt completely safe. He gave the railing a good shake to make sure it was sturdy before leaning over to have a look at the stacks of hay and boxes of stuff down below. It was a very long way down.

He'd come up here to have a look out the window, so that's just what he did. He couldn't see much. The windows were thickly covered with dust and cobwebs. In the fading sunlight he couldn't make out much more than the colors in the sky.

He took one of the arm covers off the sofa and wiped a pane clean. It was amazing. Matt pushed his face to the glass, and gazed over the golden countryside. He could see for miles. Farms, woods, barns and houses stretched out before him. He could see the concession roads scrape brown lines through the rolling countryside.

He plopped down into the rocking chair and took in the skyline. He figured that he knew why somebody would want to sit up here and rock. It was beautiful.

He could also see that the sun was near setting. Layer upon layer of orange clouds told him it would be dark in half an hour. Matt didn't have long to check out the loft before nightfall. He wasn't looking forward to the trip down, and didn't want to have to do it in the pitch dark.

He stood at the rail and looked up to the top of the barn, still a long way above him. At the height of the peak was a rope tied to the barn's center beam. The other end of the rope was fastened to a wardrobe near the far end of the platform. What would anybody want with a rope up here? he wondered. Nobody would have any reason to climb to the ceiling. It didn't make any sense. But then what did make sense up here? Who lived up here, and why? How did they get all this stuff up here?

Matt knew he'd have plenty of time to figure it out when he was back on terra firma. Maybe he wouldn't tell anybody about this place. Maybe not even Sanji. His mother would have a fit if she knew he'd climbed that ladder up here. Maybe it was a good idea to keep this under his hat for a while.

When he bent to open the trap door, he noticed the lock was spring-loaded. He climbed back onto the ladder, slipped the screwdriver back onto its shelf, and pulled the door closed. The bolt snapped into place, and he made his way carefully down the long ladder to the barn floor.

On his way out of the barn, he passed the door to the huge shed built onto the side. A big old iron lock hung on the hasp. Matt figured he could make short work of the lock, but right now it was getting dark, and his mom would be home any minute. But he was feeling different about the farm now. It was a long way from his old home in Kitchener, but it definitely had possibilities.

4

A Hunk of Junk

The hot sun woke him up. Matt had been dreaming about his school. Mr. Harding called him to the front of the room to explain a mathematical problem of speeding locomotives and the distance between towns. Flecks of dust danced in the sharp swords of sunlight spilling between the curtains. His first thought was to bounce out of bed and into his school clothes. Then it all came flooding back to him.

He didn't go to Our Lady of Mount Carmel school any more. Blood rushed to his head, bubbling with pictures of yellow school buses and big country kids wearing goofy overalls and John Deere caps. He fought with his fear of the unknown school term just two months away. He watched the dust tumble and swirl in the light and tried not to think about what lay ahead of him.

He could hear his mother downstairs, singing along with the radio. "Oh what a beautiful mo-or-or-ning, Oh what a beautiful day. I've got a wonderful fee-e-ling, everything's goin' my way!"

Yeah, Matt thought. Everything was going her way. She had a house where she wanted it, she didn't have to go to Waterloo County High, and she didn't have to mow all this grass, either. She'd already told him it was his job to keep the acre of lawn mowed. He was really starting to resent her having everything her way.

He moped along the hallway to the purple bathroom, turned on the shower, and stepped into the half-hearted drizzle of hot water.

29

Then he remembered his discovery of yesterday. He hadn't had much time to investigate, but now he had all day. And there was that locked door that needed busting open.

He toweled himself off and pulled his bed together. He knew that the Neat Freak would be up here within half an hour, and she'd be calling him from wherever he was to make his bed. He had learned that if he at least pulled the cover over the pillow she would give him a break.

Matt pulled on his old Reeboks and his Rolling Stones Review tee shirt, and made for the kitchen. He could smell toast, and wanted to get there before she packed up the breakfast stuff and scoured the kitchen.

"Well, look who's up," she teased, "Rip Van Winkle! I thought you were going to sleep 'til noon. What have you got on for the day?"

"I dunno. I thought I'd organize the stuff in the barn. There's a lot of work to do out there. I don't think the grass needs to be cut yet, and Sanji said he'd help me with it on the weekend."

"Wow, you're going to work? Voluntarily? I was going to ask if you wanted to come into Kitchener with me. I'll be picking up Sanji at around five, and I'll bring home a pizza from the Trading Post on my way home. You could hang around the park while I'm working."

He did want to go into Kitchener and watch the guys at ball practice. On the other hand, he figured there was too much to explore here. He'd have the whole day to himself. "Naw, I've got a lot to do here, Mom. I think I'll take a pass."

"Okay. Suit yourself. Anyway, I've got to run. I'm supposed to be at the office for an eleven o'clock meeting, and I wanted to stop at Costa's on the way through Fergus." She bent over the table, where Matt was scooping up a bowl of granola, and planted a smack on his forehead. "I'll see you later. Don't get into anything you shouldn't."

The screen door banged behind her, and seconds later swung open. "I forgot my briefcase! I'd look pretty stupid showing up at the meeting without this stuff." The back door banged again, and he heard her grinding down the driveway. Two minutes later, he heard tires on the driveway again. What did she forget now? Matt thought to himself. Why is it that these people make all the decisions? She can't even get out of the house for a meeting! How come she gets to run my life?

When he looked out the screen door, he didn't see his mother's Toyota, he saw Costa's black pickup truck. And her brother, he thought, is out here visiting when he's supposed to be at his store making money. These adults are amazing. They bump around their lives, buying houses and stores, and they can't figure out whether they're coming or going, and they are supposed to make decisions for me! It's ridiculous!

"Hey, Costa, what are you doin' out here? Haven't you got a business to run?" He thought it was the kind of smart remark Costa would appreciate. But the look on Costa's face told him he was wrong.

"Yeah. A business to run." Matt stepped aside as Costa slouched across the threshold. "Where's your mother?" he said, opening the refrigerator door.

"Well she's not in the fridge!" Matt's uncle could never enter a kitchen without peering into the refrigerator, and Matt had always thought it was a strange habit for a fat guy. Didn't he know that's how fat people got fat? "She's gone into Kitchener. She's probably at the Trading Post about now, knocking at the door, wondering where you are."

"Well, she'll see it then. I won't have to tell her." He put a cup of coffee into the microwave and beeped it into action. "The store is for sale."

"For sale! What are you talking about? Why are you selling the Trading Post? Who would buy it?" Matt had thought Costa was a little dim when it came to business, but he didn't think he'd sell his store without at least talking to Maria about it first. "Why would you sell the store?"

"I'm not selling it! Richard Gaston is selling it." He plunked down into a chair, put his elbows on the table and his head between his hands.

"Who's Richard Gaston?" Matt asked. This was getting complicated.

"Richard Gaston owns the building. I rent it from him. He came in this morning with a real estate guy from Toronto, and they measured up the place from stem to stern. He wants to sell the building and move to Florida. His wife has arthritis or something, and he wants to get rid of everything and move south. I've got three months left on the lease, and this real estate guy figures he can sell the building to McDonalds. So I'm out. Unless I can come up with two hundred thousand bucks."

"Two hundred thousand dollars for the Trading Post. No problem Costa! Nobody will pay that kind of money for that place!" Matt laughed. "You could buy half the downtown strip of Fergus for two hundred grand!"

He thought it was kind of funny, but he could tell that Costa was really upset. His eyes were glassed over, like he was going to cry, so Matt thought he'd better not make fun of him right now. "Does this guy really think McDonalds wants to open up a place in Fergus?"

"Yup. The two hundred thousand, two hundred and twenty thousand, to be exact, is for the Trading Post and Millie's Ladies Wear next door. Well, for the property, anyway. They'd pull the whole place down, and build from scratch. Golden arches, parking lot and drive-up counter."

He couldn't remember Costa ever being this upset before, and he noticed something else: Costa smelled bad. He'd been smoking. Costa hadn't smoked a cigarette in two years. But today, he had a pack in his shirt pocket. This was serious.

"So," his uncle continued, "I've either got to find big bucks or give up the Trading Post. Good luck, eh, nephew? You want to lend me some money? Nobody else is going to lend me that kind of money for a junk store."

"Well, if I had it I would. But I'm a kid, remember. I could lend you five bucks, but two hundred grand is a little out of my league." Matt thought about whether he'd lend that kind of money to a guy like Costa. Maybe he would, but only because he was his uncle. If he had two hundred thousand dollars, Matt figured he could find a better investment. But he wasn't going into that right now. Costa was too upset to joke around.

"Maybe" Matt continued, "we could sell this place and move in with you! You and mom paid nearly a hundred thousand for the farm, right? Why don't you sell it and we could all live in the apartment over the Trading Post? I could help run the store."

"I don't think so Matt. Nice try, though. Even if we could sell this place, we couldn't pay the mortgage and live on what I make at the Trading Post. It's impossible. Look, I've gotta go. Tell Maria to call me when she gets home. And tell Sanji we're gonna have to forget about the garage sale. If there's gonna be a sale, it's gonna be a goin' out of business sale." Costa slunk out the door and muttered his way down the steps. He lit up a cigarette and slammed the truck's door shut.

Matt watched Costa's black pickup roll down the drive and pull out onto the highway. "There goes my summer," he thought gloomily. "First they move me into the wilderness, then I lose the only thing that made me want to stay here." He dropped his bowl into the sink and glugged down another glass of milk. He couldn't believe that anybody would pay that much money for the Trading Post, but he knew that most adults weren't too bright. Most of them were like dumb kids — except they had money. Maybe somebody would be stupid enough to buy up the land for a hamburger joint.

In the barn, he was faced with a stack of cardboard boxes marked "GARAGE" and he started sorting through them, looking for the ones with tools inside. He came up with just what he wanted: a hammer and a tire iron, the great persuaders.

He set down the tire iron, and smacked the hammer gently into the palm of his hand. The lock on the shed door looked pretty solid, but he figured he could open it with one great whack. He stood there looking at the door, and with the morning light streaming in, he could see that something was painted across it. He could make out a 'W', 'BA' and 'CO', but the rest was faded and covered with dust and dirt. He gave the lock a slam with the hammer. Nothing. Two more great cracks of the hammer had the same result, so he got out the heavy artillery. He jiggled the tire iron into the lock loop and pulled with all his might. Nothing. He re-set the tool and gave it another go. More of the same: nothing.

Matt wondered if there was any dynamite in the boxes. He'd need something pretty serious to get into that shed. There were no windows in the building, and it looked as solid as a vault. He put his head back, scanning the rafters from end to end.

He remembered something he'd seen up in the loft. On the bookshelf was a set of keys, sitting in a saucer. It was obvious. One of those keys would open this lock!

He swung himself up onto the rungs and climbed hand-over-hand. From his position high up on the ladder, he could see across to the other deck. There didn't seem to be anything up there except a few large wooden crates. But there was no way to get over there. He could see no trace of a ladder long enough to reach the loft. He reached the loose rung and pulled himself past without stepping on it. He wondered if whoever built this place left it loose to eliminate intruders. It was a long drop from here.

Once up on the deck, he went straight for the key ring. There were about twenty keys on it, and he jangled them into his pocket and slipped back down onto the ladder.

The first three keys went into the lock, but none of them turned. The next two didn't look even close, but the sixth one slipped in smoothly and with a twist of the wrist, released the hasp. The lock was free, but the door still wouldn't budge. Matt rattled the knob, pounded the wooden door with his shoulder, and whacked at it with the tire iron. He was no closer to the inside of the shed than he had been an hour ago.

He was ready to rethink the whole thing, when his eyes landed on the solution. About five paces along from the door was another lock, just at ground level. He scrambled over and jabbed key after key into the lock. It wasn't long before he found the one he wanted. With a click the lock turned cleanly and dropped into his hand. He grabbed the iron handle on the side of the barn and gave it a shove. It opened a crack, and he knew how it worked now. The door to the shed was cut into the center of a larger sliding door.

He slipped the tire iron into the crack and gave a mighty pull. The entire wall began to move. He dropped the iron and slid his hands into the narrow opening. With his feet against a post he stretched his legs out, forcing the wall to open. The panel creaked and groaned, yielding a little, and he slithered inside.

How he could have thought this was a shed was impossible for him to figure. From the outside, this add-on to the barn looked small and dark, but from the inside, it was massive, with light flooding in through a skylight. The shed was nearly half the size of the barn itself. He looked over the mechanics of the door. The entire wall was made to roll back, making a huge opening into the barn.

The room was empty, except for a curious hunk of metal which stood in the center. It was some kind of old machine, covered with flaking paint.

What the heck is this? Matt whistled to himself. The machine was the size of a hay wagon and had huge claws and long arms along each side. There were pedals on each flank, in the shape of large feet, and levers along the side at short intervals. At each of the corners was a crank and a dial under dirty glass, with needles all pointing to zero.

The main body of the machine was solid iron. The top was completely flat, with two rows of rollers laying side by side along the entire length. Matt examined the machine from top to bottom, trying to figure out what it was for.

It looked like something out of a crummy Saturday afternoon Frankenstein film. He could imagine a mad scientist pulling the levers and turning the cranks, and a stumbling monster in the grip of the mighty claw arms. But what was it really for? This was even stranger than the living area up in the loft!

He tried pulling on the levers, but they were rusted fast. The cranks were pretty much stuck, too, but one seemed to give a little, so he slipped out of the shed to get a hammer. He gave the crank a tap and it swung free. He turned it first this way, and then that, but it didn't do anything. It didn't seem to connect to anything else. Just a crank that cranked nothing. He tapped on each of the levers, stepped on the pedals and cleaned off the glass dials. Nothing explained what this thing was for, and none of it did anything.

At one end of the machine was an engine. Matt knew a little about engines, and it seemed to be some sort of modified car or truck motor with a gear shift hooked to the side. There was a lever with a round red knob on the end, which had to be the accelerator. The red knob was the only thing which still had any paint left on it. The whole machine was covered with flakes of old paint, and rust. The knob was red and shiny. He ran his fingers over it, wondering. He tried the gear shift on the left, but it was frozen stiff by the rust.

Matt looked around the barn for clues. There were more puzzles in this barn than there were pieces to fit together. In the corner was a large wooden platform with a winching system built onto it. "Yes!" he hooted. "That's how he got all that stuff up to the deck! He used a pulley system. This is an elevator!" He climbed up on the platform and carefully examined the motor and mechanical system. There was no question of what this was. He crossed over to the door and poked his head through the opening, looking up into the rafters of the barn. The other end of the pulley was still up there. Maybe he could get this thing working!

Feeling very intelligent, he returned to the huge machine and kicked it, hoping this might make it give up its secret. He gave the red knob a pull. It moved like a hot knife through butter. The ground under his feet began to vibrate, and sparks shot out from the motor. The massive machine began to growl and hum, then it began to rattle and shake ferociously.

BAARRAAP! ZIGGAAP! HUNK HUNK HUNK BAARRAAP! The motor jumped to life! In a panic, Matt shot a glance at the dial to his left and saw that the needle had jumped to three, and the claw arms started to rattle and creak. The rollers ground into action, and in a second were spinning at an incredible rate. The claws began to clack in place. The elbow joints squawked and flexed. Enough was enough. He was terrified. He grabbed the red knob and tried to pull it back. It was completely stuck. Matt yanked at it in desperation. The huge machine roared angrily, grinding and snapping, sparks flying from the screaming engine.

He skipped to the far side of the motor, looking to yank the wire from the rusty spark plug. One of the claw arms swung around, clacking and snapping at his head. He ducked out of its swinging path, and watched it snap its powerful jaws in the air. He made for the spark plug again, but this time he heard snapping jaws behind him. He covered his head with one hand and reached for the spark plug with the other.

The claw arm swept through the air, snapping ferociously, and whacked him on the head, sending him sprawling face first into the dirt. As he went down, he thought of what his mother would say. "I thought I told you not to get up to anything you shouldn't!" He saw her brown eyes frowning at him, her red lips calling out to him, and the world spun around and went black.

The blanket of blackness covered the boy completely. Dream images danced and swayed through his jumbled head. His father stood before him, smiling. Then, lying still and dead in his coffin, his father smiled at him again. He saw Sanji on the mound, shaking off signals while Matt furiously flashed for the fastball. The pictures swam before him, spinning into a tornado of faces and feelings. Matt spun into a dream world which no longer made any sense at all.

The whirling images began to slow down and take shape. In his dream's eye, Matt saw a boy, long and thin, with dirty overalls and hair the color of straw, lying face down in the dirt. Though he somehow knew it was a dream, for Matt it was all very real.

The dream-boy began to stir. He reached back, rubbed his head, and sputtered a mouthful of dirt into the sawdust on the floor.

He opened his eyes and heard the thumping of the machine. He turned his blonde head, saw the red arms waving in the air, the green handles moving back and forth of their own accord. Incredible stacks of rough-hewn lumber, rolls of leather, and giant crates filled most of the barn. He shook himself and rose to his knees. He held his head with both hands, trying to muffle the sound of the roaring machine and coddle his aching noggin at the same time.

"Hannibal's elephants, Ol' Man Wagner's gonna kill me!" he sputtered. "I got to get out of here!" Jimmy scrambled to his feet and made for the barn door. He crept around the side so as not to be seen. Hanging on a nail near the door of the workshop was a black and tan jackknife. He'd seen one of these before. It was exactly the kind Ralph Otis had. He pulled it open and snapped it shut, then slipped it into his pocket, and made a dash for the door.

"JIMMY FOX YOU HOOLIGAN, I'LL HAVE A WORD WITH YOUR FATHER, YOU YOUNG SO AND SO!" roared Ol' Man Wagner, and was after him like a shot. Jimmy was fast. He knew he could outrun nearly everybody in the county, so this old guy would be no problem. He jumped the fence in one bound and was across the field and nearly home before he knew it.

5

Ol' Man Wagner

"**I**'ve seen him! I've seen him!" Jimmy hissed to his kid brother, Hal. "I seen Ol' Man Wagner! I got into the barn, and there was this huge machine, you won't believe what he's got in there! It's like nothin'! There's stacks of lumber, rolls of stuff, and... you should see what he's got in there!"

Jimmy's dad had told the boys to stay clear of Mr. Wagner. The talk was that he was crazy as a loon, and probably up to no good. Some said he was an American outlaw, some said he was just a harmless old coot, but everybody agreed that he was somebody to steer clear of.

Although Ol' Man Wagner had moved into the Thompson place two years ago, hardly anyone had seen him. During the day, trucks from all over had made deliveries to the farm, and often at night there were lamps burning well into the wee hours.

"Did he see you?" Hal asked, his eyes wide with amazement.

"See me? He chased me halfway across the field, waving a stick and yelling! And he's some kind of fast for an old guy! I just made it over the fence ahead of him."

Jimmy was about to whip out the knife he'd stolen from the barn, but then he thought better of it. He wasn't sure why he'd taken it in the first place. He couldn't show anybody without admitting to stealing it, and he wasn't keen on telling people he was a thief.

Hal went downstairs to see if supper was ready. Jimmy lay on his bed, thinking about the things he had seen at Ol' Man Wagner's place.

The bedroom door swung open and Hal burst in, breathless. "Jimmy, you're in for it! Ol' Man Wagner was just here!"

"Here! You mean at our house?" Jimmy groaned in disbelief.

"Yep, and he had a talk with Ma and Pa. Looks like you're in for it now, Jimmy. Pa looked real worried when Ol' Man Wagner left. He and ma are still talkin' in the kitchen."

Hal scrambled up the ladder to Jimmy's bed and spilled out a handful of jacks. "I bet you're gonna die by tomorrow," Hal said, scooping up two of the jacks. "Can I have your hockey stick after they kill you?" He scooped up three jacks this time, leaving two on the bed.

Jimmy shoved Hal over and chucked the rest of the jacks onto the floor. "You better git, or you'll be in it with me." Hal jumped over the edge, grabbed up the jacks and looked down the hallway.

Hal was eight. Like Jimmy, he had hair the color of straw and a great imagination. Unlike Jimmy, Hal had something to say about everything. He couldn't stand to hear the sound of silence, and filled up any empty space with the sound of his voice. It was good to have him around, though. It gave Jimmy somebody to blame.

Hal stuck his head out the bedroom window and scanned the yard. "If you're gonna make a getaway, now's the time!"

"Jimmy!" his father called from the bottom of the stairs.

"Too late, Jimmy," Hal warned.

"Yes sir, I'm comin'." Jimmy shrugged his shoulders and slouched along the hallway and down to the kitchen. His mother was standing at the sink, and his father sat at the table with a cup of coffee between his hands. There were two more cups out on the table and one of them was empty. Hal hadn't been kidding. Somebody had been here.

"Jimmy, sit down," said his father. "Ma, maybe you better sit down, too." He didn't seem mad. Maybe Hal was kidding. Maybe somebody else was here; maybe it wasn't Ol' Man Wagner at all.

"Jimmy, what are the two places you're not allowed to go around here?" Yep, thought Jimmy Fox, Ol' Man Wagner was here.

"The railroad tracks, sir." He always called his pa 'sir'. And especially when he was in trouble.

"And?" Wil Fox gulped his coffee and stared at the boy. He knew what had gone on this afternoon, but he wanted Jimmy to tell the story himself. He had tried hard to teach his boys to tell the truth and he expected Jimmy to do so now.

"... And the Thompson Place. The railroad tracks and the Thompson Place." Jimmy wasn't going to lie about anything, but he wasn't going to add any details he wasn't asked for. There was no point making this any worse than it already was. Had Ol' Man Wagner missed his jackknife?

"So where were you this afternoon, when you were supposed to be mending the fence?"

"I was... well I was following King, sir. He just headed over the fields toward the Thompson Place, and I just sort of went along the side of the barn, and the door was open, so I just looked in. I didn't mean any trouble, I just saw all that stuff, so I thought I'd just look around. I didn't think he'd see me, Pa. I was just gonna stay for a minute."

"Go on." Wil looked over at his wife, Irma. He wasn't smiling, but inside, he was rather proud of Jimmy for having told the truth.

"Well, he's got this huge machine in there. It's silver and green and black, and it's got arms and things, and rollers, and I just wanted to take a look at it. And then it started up all by itself! I didn't touch it, it just started groaning and thumping! And something smacked me from behind, and knocked me down. When I got up, the machine had stopped, and I was kind of dizzy. And then I saw Ol' Man, I mean, Mr. Wagner, and he started yelling at me, so I just took off." He thought about the jackknife. Maybe he should tell about the knife too. But he was already in enough trouble.

"Jimmy, how many times has your father told you to stay away from the Thompson Place?" His mother seemed madder than his father did. She kept looking from Jimmy to his dad and back to Jimmy.

"A few, I reckon. I never went there before. It was just because of the dog, ma. I didn't mean to do it. I was just makin' sure King didn't get into any trouble."

"Jimmy, Mr. Wagner was here a little while ago. He says he chased you across the field, calling for you to stop." Finally, Jimmy could tell that his father wasn't too angry. It was the way he said "Jimmy". If he had said "James Wilson" or "James Wilson Fox" or even "Jimmy Fox", he'd have known it was serious, but "Jimmy" usually meant the worst was over.

"I couldn't stop, pa, I thought he'd kill me. He's a Yankee outlaw, ya know! I don't know what he'd have done if he'd caught me. And he nearly did. Ol' Man Wagner can *run*."

"It's a very good thing for you that he's not an outlaw, Jimmy. No matter what people say, he is our neighbor, and we'll think the best of him." He stood up and put his arm around Irma's shoulders and smiled at Jimmy and at Hal, who had snuck into the kitchen. "He's peculiar, to be sure, but I don't think he's an outlaw. Anyway, he's giving you a chance to make up for trespassing. He wants you to be at his place at six-thirty tomorrow morning, ready to work. He says he's never seen a boy move across a field as fast as you did, and he could use a strong boy to do some chores."

"Chores?" Jimmy repeated, fearfully. "At Ol' Man Wagner's place? What about the fence? I ain't finished fixing the fence yet, pa."

"Fixing the fence! You weren't too eager to fix our fence this afternoon." Wil Fox was smiling. Irma was smiling too.

"You take a lunch with you, Jimmy," she said. "I've got a feeling you'll be a busy boy tomorrow." His mother pulled her red hair back over her brow. "I'd say you'd better get yourself to bed early, Sonny Jim."

At six-fifteen the next morning, Jimmy slipped through the fence and stood outside Ol' Man Wagner's barn. He had the knife in his back pocket. He'd hoped to find some way to get it back into the workshop without the old man seeing him. "Mr. Wagner?" he called into the barn. There was no answer, so he pushed the door open.

The door to the workshop was partly open, and nobody was around. "Mr. Wagner?" he called, this time a little louder.

"That ch'ew, boy?" Jimmy jumped at the raspy sound of Ol' Man Wagner's voice. "I'll be out'n a minute, boy. Just you wait for me there. An' stay out of the barn!" Jimmy looked around, but he couldn't figure out where the voice was coming from. The outhouse maybe?

He felt for the knife in his back pocket. It would take only a minute to run into the barn, put the knife back where he found it, and he'd be back out here before the old man had time to see him. He started for the door.

"D'you hear me, boy? You stay out of that barn 'til I git finished!" came the twang from nowhere.

There was no way he was going to get the knife back into the barn. He shrugged, picked up a small rock and launched it at a crow on the fence. He missed by a mile, but the crow fluttered off anyway. He picked up another and threw it at the bird as it arched upward and away from the barn. He wasn't even close.

"Heee! What're you doin' boy?" Jimmy nearly jumped out of his boots. Ol' Man Wagner was standing right behind him. "What d'ya call that? You call that throwin'?"

He spun around, and there was Ol' Man Wagner. He looked a lot bigger close up. He was taller than Jimmy's dad by a good bit, and he didn't look so old from here. He was buttoning his overalls and had a toothpick dancing between his lips.

"I was just... just throwin' a rock, sir."

"That's not throwin', boy, this is throwin'." Mr. Wagner picked up a rock and whipped it up at the top of the barn. It hit the weathervane with a loud "Dong!", bounced off the rooster, and spun off in the direction of the high flying crow. "Caw" screamed the crow, leaving tail feathers drifting down to the ground. "Wow!" yelped Jimmy.

"Now, that my boy, is throwin' rocks.

"Take this pail, and put it on the stump yonder, boy." He pointed to a tree stump across the field, near the garden. Jimmy ran over, set the bucket in place, and ran back to where the man was lugging a sack of potatoes.

"Here, boy, throw one of these spuds and knock that can off the stump."

Jimmy figured he had to be kidding. The can was about twice as far away as he could possibly throw a potato. He heaved the spud with all his might, and got it to fly and roll about two-thirds of the way to the pail.

"Ha, ha, ha. Great, boy, now watch this." Wagner handed Jimmy an armload of potatoes. "You toss 'em to me, boy." And with that, he threw the first potato high into the air. "Come on, come on, keep 'em comin!" Jimmy tossed another spud to the old man, he grabbed it in mid-air, and in one motion launched it at the pail, grabbing the next and the next spud, faster than Jimmy could toss them to him. The potatoes arched high, nearly out of sight before heading straight down to the ground.

Twang! The first spud landed in the pail. Twang, twang, twang, twang, rang the next four. "Now, here's the kicker, boy!" He wound up and pitched one straight across the field just as the last of the arching 'taters was plunking down into the can. Jimmy tried to follow it, but the spud flew too fast for him to see.

Barrang! It smacked the pail clean off the stump and into the air, spilling the potatoes all over the garden.

"Holy cow! That's... It's fantasticle!" Jimmy stood marvelling. He grabbed a potato out of the sack and heaved it in the direction of the bucket. He nearly got it as far as the stump this time, and he heard the old man laughing at him. "Here, boy, try this. Ya grip it across here," he said, spreading Jimmy's fingers out, bending them into the correct potato grip. "Now, don't throw it overhand, swipe your arm way back, and launch it with your wrist, like this," he tossed one off, grunting, "so it never goes higher than your shoulder. And look at the way my feet are. That's right," he said, planting the boy's feet properly in the dirt. "Now, give it a toss." Jimmy hauled back and threw the potato. He didn't hit the stump, but it was further than he'd ever thrown anything before. He couldn't believe it.

"There. That's lesson number one. I'll give ya lesson number two when ya get all these potatoes planted in the garden. Now, go

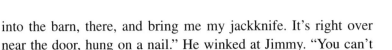

into the barn, there, and bring me my jackknife. It's right over near the door, hung on a nail." He winked at Jimmy. "You can't miss it, boy."

Jimmy ran to the barn and came back with the jackknife, handing it to the enormous old man. "Now, boy, let's get a few things straight. My name is Albertus J. Wagner. You can call me Butts. When I call you, you stop what you're doin' and answer me. No more running away. I could probably catch you anyway, if I wanted to. Ain't many people faster'n me, and none of them are twelve years old."

He handed the knife back to Jimmy. "I want you to cut these taters in half, and plant 'em flat side down in hills, three feet apart. When you're done, come back up to the barn and I'll give you twenty-five cents. You know how to plant taters, James? "

"Yes sir, I've done it with my Ma," Jimmy stuttered. His head was still reeling from the trick with the potatoes and from the mention of twenty-five cents. Twenty-five cents for planting a sack of potatoes? He'd heard that all Americans were rich, and now he believed it! Who'd pay twenty-five cents for planting one sack of spuds? He must be crazy!

The old man turned and headed for the barn, leaving Jimmy with a gigantic sack of potatoes and the jackknife.

6

Fast Ground and Short Hops

Planting a whole sack of potatoes was a long and dirty job, but Jimmy was used to hard work. He dug and planted in a fury, rows neat and straight like his mother had taught him, scurrying back and forth with pails full of soggy spuds and water from the well. He wanted to investigate the strange noises coming from inside the barn. He could hear buzzing and clanking, whining and thumping and the occasional yelp, as if someone had hit their thumb with a hammer. The barn doors were closed up tight, so he couldn't see what was going on in there, but he knew something strange was happening. The sooner he finished with the potatoes, the sooner he could find out what it was.

He kept looking back at the enormous red barn. He felt as though he were being watched, but there was never anyone around when he looked. Once, he thought he saw something move in the upper windows. He figured it was a pigeon or something, but still he kept looking back up to see if anything was moving up there.

He filled the pail with potatoes and water for about the hundredth time. The bag was light enough to drag along now, so he slung it over his shoulder and trudged out to the far end of the field.

Jimmy swung the sack to the ground and looked back to the barn again. It was a big barn, even for around here. And unlike most barns, it had a row of huge windows up high. He was sure he'd seen something move up there more than once. He held up his hand to block the sun, running his eyes along the blazing glass. There it was again! Something *had* moved up there! He'd get a closer look when he was done. He poured out a pail full of spidery, soft potatoes and set to work cutting them up and digging them into the soil.

He wiped his dirty hands on his trousers, and looked over the rows of potato hills. The sun was well past mid-day. He figured he'd done a good day's work, but it was hardly worth twenty-five cents. He stumped over to the barn and swung the door wide. The sound inside was deafening. He covered his ears, and swung his eyes around the vast, bright room. The machine that had whacked him sat in the center of the large workshop. It was silent, but menacing, with its long pincher arms that could catch a guy from behind.

He cupped his hands around his mouth to shout above the whining of the motor. "Mr. Wagner!" he called, searching the piles of lumber, rolls and crates.

The old man yelled back, "Done already?" The boy spun around, startled, searching for him. "Must have been a small sack of potatoes." Jimmy's head craned back and he looked up.

There, dangling in the sunbeams above his head, was Ol' Man Wagner, slowly gliding down from the heights of the barn, on a square wooden skid. Jimmy was stunned into silence. Ol' Man Wagner, floating and grinning like some cranky angel, descended from on high. Closer and closer he drifted on his gently swaying skid, smiling ear to ear, with his toothpick jumping around in his mouth.

Next to him on the skid was the source of the racket. A motor, roaring away, turned a long rope and pulley, letting the rope out smoothly as he coasted nearer the floor. The old man pulled a lever, slowing the skid and lowering the volume of noise.

Jimmy looked up to where the ropes were tied. Way up above the loft was the center beam which held up the roof of the barn. Four or five ropes were wrapped around it and two of them were attached to the motor. The skid itself had rails around three sides and except for the fact that it moved it looked like a small porch without steps.

"Ya never seen an elevator before, boy?" Jimmy stood with his mouth open, staring at the man and the unbelievable machine. He'd never seen anything like this 'elevator' before.

"Now, let's have a look at your potato planting, James." Jimmy headed toward the door, and he heard Ol' Man Wagner chuckling behind him.

"Where'ya goin', James? I said let's go have a look at the potato field." Jimmy looked back at the old man still standing on the skid. "Come on, boy, climb aboard!"

"Ya mean you want me to go up there," he pointed to the loft "on that thing?" Jimmy's heart thumped and his hands started sweating. He hoped the old man was kidding.

"Well, you could climb the ladder over there, but what good is American ingenuity if you don't use it? Suit yerself." The engine roared and the skid began to rise slowly off the floor. Jimmy had to scramble aboard, making it sway wildly back and forth, but he was soon standing next to Ol' Man Wagner, holding on to the side rail for dear life as the elevator climbed upward.

"Did you build this thing yourself, Mr. Wagner?" Jimmy asked.

The old man jerked the accelerator and frowned at the boy. "I told you. Call me Butts. And yes, I built it myself. It's no trick, boy. Elevators are the coming thing. There's nothing like it compared to walkin'!

"The engine turns the flywheel here, and this is the accelerator. Makes it go faster. I'm thinkin' about re-jiggin' the whole thing, ya know, put the motor on the ground, and run a long cable to it. I dunno. Doesn't seem to be a lot of sense in movin' the motor up and down when I only wanna move the *load* up and down."

As they approached the loft, Jimmy could see that it was a lot bigger than he'd imagined. The engine slowed to a groan, and the skid came to a stop alongside an opening in the railing.

"Just step over quickly while I tie her up, boy," Butts said, switching off the machine.

Jimmy stepped off the swaying elevator, very glad to be off the contraption and onto something solid. Butts followed him and tied the elevator to the rail.

"Welcome to my home, James."

"Your *home*?" Jimmy was flabbergasted. "You mean you *live* up here?"

"Oh, yessir, I live up here all right. All the comforts of home." He took a fresh toothpick from a small white cup on the table. The cup was white with a blue, red and gold baseball diamond painted on the side. The handle was three baseball bats with gold rings around the handles.

Butts Wagner walked over to the long wall of windows which looked out over the countryside. "Once I came up here and saw this view, I figured there was no sense in wasting it. So I put in these windows. And that's why I built the elevator. No sense in climbing all those stairs. I moved everything up here ages ago. I guess I know every inch of the township by now. I know when your daddy's crops are ready before he does, and I've seen you and your young brother sneak out at night more than once. What's his name, Herbert?"

"No, Harold, er, Hal... You mean you seen us sneak out and you never told?"

"It ain't none of my business. If you two kids want to git yerselves in trouble, well, I've been a kid myself..." He smiled at Jimmy and winked. "Just don't be gettin into what you shouldn't and I'll keep what I know to myself... You done a pretty good job with that garden, James. Look here, the rows are all straight and tidy."

Jimmy looked way down to where he had been working. The tiny hills of fresh dirt were all in neat rows, and he felt pretty good about his day's work. He put his hands in his back pockets and felt the jackknife in the left side. "Oh, here's you knife, Mr. Wagner," he said, holding the wonderful little tool out for his new friend.

"You better keep it, boy, you and that potato knife have got a lot of doin' before you're done... And call me Butts!"

"Okay, Butts," he said awkwardly.

Butts flicked a silver coin across to Jimmy. It was an American twenty-five-cent piece. "Here's your quarter, James. Ya did a good day's work, boy. If ya squeeze it real hard, that eagle's supposed to grin."

"Soda, James?" Butts reached his arm into a washtub full of water, and came up with a bottle of Coca Cola. He winked at Jimmy and handed him the unopened bottle. Jimmy wasn't sure how to open it. He'd seen Mr. Patterson open bottles at the store in town, but he'd never done it himself, and he didn't think Ol' Man Wagner was going to have one of those opening gadgets up here anyway.

"The knife, boy, use the knife!" the old man snorted. "Here, give it to me."

Jimmy handed him the knife, and watched closely as Butts put the tip of the blade under the tin cap and pried it all around. He handed Jimmy the bottle, and opened one for himself.

Butts drained his pop in a flash and put the empty bottle on the table. He nodded to Jimmy and stepped out onto the elevator.

"There'll be another twenty-five cents if you come back tomorrow. And lesson number two is how to throw straight. By the end of the week, I'll have you throwin' taters from one end of the garden t'other! Tossin' taters is about the best baseball practice you can get."

Jimmy stepped out onto the dangling platform and held on tightly. Butts pulled the rope free and started up the engine. He spoke loudly, over the din of the motor. "D'ya ever play baseball around here, boy?"

"Yes sir, Mr., ah, Butts. The Fergus Lions play all around the county." He remembered the time he went with Ralph Otis to try out for the team. Neither he nor Ralph made the first cut at the tryout. "I'm not one for baseball, I'm more of a hockey player..."

"Hockey! *Cyclone Taylor*, now there's a hockey player! I've played a bit of hockey too, back home in Pittsburgh. You know, Pittsburgh's a hockey town. Yessiree. I've had the blades on and scored a few on the rink. But that Cyclone Taylor, why he's the best hockey player who ever lived! I met him one time in New York. A heck of a nice guy, that Cyclone Taylor.

"I'll tell you something about Cyclone Taylor. When he was a boy in Saskatchewan he learned how to skate from a carnival skater, a figure skater, and he learned how to skate backwards. And then he could skate backwards better than anybody else could skate forwards! So he was always switchin' around, back to front, back to front, like a cyclone, ya see. And you know, James, that Cyclone Taylor was the highest paid athlete of his day, because he did things differently to anybody else. He did something, well, revolutionary! There's a lesson in that..." The spinning toothpick paused as Butts dropped the elevator lightly to the ground.

When Jimmy arrived the next morning, he was completely unprepared for what he saw. The entire field beside the garden had been transformed overnight. There was a broad circle of fresh brown dirt just beyond the barn wall. In the center of the circle was a smooth leather mat — home plate. The base-lines began a few long steps out from each corner of the plate, and were marked by crisp whitewash lines in the short grass.

Butts was nowhere to be seen. Jimmy walked along the side of the barn and plopped down on a newly placed bench. He looked out at the straight white lines where whitewashed hopsack bases marked first and third, and up the gentle slope in front to the pitcher's mound. Jimmy had seen real baseball diamonds before. He'd been to games in Berlin, and Waterloo, where the International League played, but he'd never seen anything quite like this. This was no town sandlot. This was a real, professional baseball diamond. And it was in Ol' Man Wagner's field! "Why in heaven does he want a baseball diamond..." he said out loud.

A voice boomed out, "It's why I bought the place, boy. It's the *ideal* baseball field."

Jimmy popped off the bench like a jack-in-the-box, spinning in the direction of the voice. He whacked his elbow on the barn wall. There was Butts Wagner, hands on his hips, toothpick flipping around in his mouth, dressed from cap to cleats in a Brooklyn Dodgers uniform. Jimmy's mouth dropped open, and he plunked back down on the bench in surprise. He couldn't take his eyes off Ol' Man Wagner.

Butts didn't notice. He was staring out over his night's work. "Y'see how the whole field is flat, James? It's perfectly level for nearly three hundred feet in all directions, except for bang dead in front of you there, where she slopes up gently for sixty-five feet, and slopes away level again." He squinted into the morning sun in right field. "All I had to do was measure off from the natural pitching mound to home plate. Sixty feet, six inches." Ol' Man Wagner was lost somewhere in his peculiar thoughts, admiring the spanking new diamond.

"This may be the finest natural playing field in the entire known world, James. The ground is solid, and fast, and the grass is green, and doesn't grow high. At game time the sun is well out of harm's way, and, being on a hill, the rain runs off quickly. This place was *made* to be a ball yard." He took off his cap and scratched his bald-and-silver head. "What d'ya think James?" He turned to Jimmy. "Ready for lesson number two?"

Jimmy nodded automatically. He climbed to his feet and rubbed his smarting elbow. He wasn't sure what to do. Ol' Man Wagner wasn't an outlaw, but he was crazy. "What d'ya mean the field is fast, Butts?"

"Well," Butts obviously enjoyed answering questions, and Jimmy put him on to his favorite topic, the science of baseball. "Y'see, a baseball, when it hits the ground, begins to slow down. The hardness or softness of the ground determines how far, and how fast, the ball will go once it hits. If, say, we were to play in your dad's fallow pasture, the ball would hit the ground, and stop right there. We'd call that a slow field. We'd call it a *dead* field. But here, where the green cover is short and stumpy, the ball will bounce and keep on goin', 'cause the ground is so hard. An infielder had better move quick to play a short-hop here..."

Jimmy understood about half of what the old man said. He wondered what a short-hop was, but he was afraid to ask.

"Ever use a glove, James?" Butts asked, bending into his brown sack. He came up rubbing a gray ball. "You haven't played much baseball, have you?"

"No, sir. We've played some at school, but not real baseball. Just sort of scrub ball..." Jimmy apologized.

"Well, today, you're gonna play baseball." He handed Jimmy a black leather glove. It was nearly flat, with fat fingers, and a solid triangle of shiny leather between the thumb and first finger. Jimmy's hand fit loosely into the worn leather slots, and he instinctively smacked his fist into the pocket.

"Let's see you catch a few, James." The old man took a bat out of the bag and set it on his shoulder. "You go out to center field, I'll hit a few out."

Jimmy jogged out behind second base and waited for the ball. The old man stood leaning on the bat waiting for him to get ready. "*Center field*, James," he called. Jimmy looked first one way, and then the other, and sure as rain, he was standing halfway between the two long foul lines. Butts shook his head and tossed the ball up into the air. When it dropped to knee level, he swooped and smacked it hard and high. As the bat came around, he shouted "I said *center field*, boy, not drawn short stop!" Jimmy watched in amazement as the ball sailed far over his head. "*That's* center field, James!"

Jimmy ran out to the ball and threw it most of the way in. The next ball dropped into his glove, as did the next and the next. Jimmy thought he was getting pretty good at this game. The next ball he had to run for, but he got it.

Pretty soon, Butts had him running this way and that to catch the thing, but he wasn't going to let the ball get away, and he didn't. Butts smacked drifting long-balls for the best part of an hour. Jimmy caught them all. He was running and wishing that Hal and Ralph Otis could see this. He knew he wasn't imagining it, but he couldn't really believe it either. And he wasn't going to let any of these balls hit the ground.

"Come on in, James. Had enough?" Butts barked from home plate.

Jimmy was just getting warmed up. He could do this all day. "Okay. You want me to hit some to *you*, Mr. Wagner?"

"I don't suppose you could hit a ball much past second base without some coaching, son. Maybe that'll be lesson number three." He leaned on the bat and mopped his brow. "Maybe you can fix that fence for me instead. I don't want any kids trespassin' y'know. And don't call me Mr. Wagner. The only Mr. Wagner I know is my daddy, and he's been dead years. It's Butts."

They headed for the barn, where Butts kept the tools for fixing fences. "You got legs, boy, I'll give you that. You could be a ball player. With the right learning. What size feet have you got there?"

"Size nine," Jimmy said, wondering why his shoe size mattered to Butts. "What is all this? I mean, why are you doing all this? Why do you have a baseball uniform and all this stuff? Why have you put this baseball diamond on your farm?" Jimmy was full of questions.

Butts broke out laughing. "Why, I guess you think I'm crazy!" He sat down on the bench, still snorting. "Maybe I *am* crazy... Yeah, that's it. I am crazy."

Butts grunted. "My whole life has been baseball, James. When I was your age, I'd been to a hundred baseball games, and I'd played in three times that many. Baseball is all I've ever known..." He wasn't laughing any more. He tipped his cap down against the sun and spun the toothpick around with his lips.

"I don't expect the name Butts Wagner to mean much up here in Canada. Oh, the baseball clubs would know it, sure, but nobody else would. Back home, in America, everybody's heard of the Wagner brothers. I ended up with the Dodgers, my brother is the star of the Pittsburgh Pirates. My kid brother is said by many to be the best shortstop that ever lived; maybe the best *player* that ever lived. The great Honus Wagner. And I taught him everything he knows. Honus Wagner..." Butts was looking up into the sky, speaking in a daze, "the greatest ball player ever..."

"He is, too." His eyes came to sudden life, flashing at Jimmy. "And I taught him everything he knows," he repeated.

"You taught the greatest player ever how to play?" Jimmy sputtered, his eyes popping, and his ears sucking up every word. "And he's your brother?" Jimmy thought of Hal, the greatest baseball player ever. He doubted it. "He plays for the Pittsburgh Pirates? I've heard of them! And you taught him? I thought you were a bank robber!" His ears burned with the thought of what he'd just said.

"A bank robber? Ha ha! I shoulda been a bank robber, it sure pays better!" Butts laughed. "If I were a bank robber, maybe people around here would have heard of me! Let's get to that fence, boy."

Butts showed him where the wood for fencing was kept, at the back of the barn, and told him not to use any of the other wood. "When yer done, just come up to the loft. And don't make too much noise about it, I'm due for a nap!"

7

Thugs

Jimmy dragged out the long planks he would need for the broken section of fence. He wondered why he wasn't supposed to use the wood from any of the other piles. They didn't look different, except that they were cleaner, and the piles were higher. He tried to lift one of the long blond planks. It was so heavy he couldn't even budge it.

The morning was nearly over, and Jimmy's stomach was rumbling. He got the lunch his mother had made for him, and went to sit on the home plate bench to eat it. She had packed a big bowl of dumplings and sauce from last night's dinner. He scooped up a forkful of potatoes and perked up his ears. A car was coming.

Jimmy set down his lunch and went to the corner of the barn, where he could see the road. A car was coming all right. And it wasn't just any car. Jimmy had seen pictures of these long wide wonders, with their dazzling chrome from top to bottom. It was a red Cadillac Sedan, an American car. It swung up the laneway toward the house. The Cadillac bumped and purred softly over the dusty lane and came to a rocking stop.

Two men sat in the front seat, and one in the back. Jimmy thought they looked like gangsters. They all wore dark hats and two of them wore their suit jackets. Jimmy figured that nobody but gangsters wore their hats and jackets at this time of day.

The purr of the engine vanished, and there was only the hiss and gurgle of the hot motor. Jimmy stayed where he was, out of sight. As much as he wanted to have a better look at the car, he had a bad feeling about this.

The doors swung open and the three men climbed out, stretching their legs and looking around. None of them said anything. Two went around to the front of the house, while the third man, who wore only a shirt and pants, a Sunday hat and suspenders, went up the back stairs and stood on the porch. They didn't look like they were on a social call.

Jimmy went to the side door of the barn, well out of sight of the three men, and knocked quietly. Nobody answered. He knocked again, and whispered loudly. "Mr. Wagner... Mr. Wagner! Lemme in!" He gave the door a shove, but it was bolted fast.

Yesterday, Jimmy had noticed the iron slots behind all the doors, and the two-by-eight planks resting on the door jambs. Butts must have set the planks into the slots. Nobody was going to get into the barn if Ol' Man Wagner didn't want them in there, and he definitely didn't want these guys in there.

"Hey, kid! Hold it, kid! Hey, Louie, there's a kid over here!" The man in the suspenders was standing at the corner of the barn. He took a few steps toward Jimmy, squinting at him, and tipped his hat to the back of his head. Jimmy knew it was too late to run, so he decided to play dumb.

"You just stay right where you are and you won't get hurt," the suspenders man growled. "Louie! Ya better get over here," he called over his shoulder.

The other two men strutted around the corner of the barn, their gleaming shoes scuffing the whitewashed baselines. "Well, well, well. Who've we got here?" Louie, the driver of the Cadillac, smiled. "How are ya'll, son? Are ya'll a friend of Mr. Wagner?" The driver turned to the third man, "Wagner don't have any kids, does he Jingo?"

"Don't think so. Probably never had time." He looked at Jimmy, sizing him up. "Naw, if Wagner had a kid, Louie, he'd be *your age* by now!"

Louie looked back to Jimmy. "You live here, boy?" he asked.

Jimmy said nothing.

"I asked you a question, nice like, boy. Let's try it again. D'yall live here?"

Jimmy just squinted back at him. He was scared skinny, but he figured the best thing to do was to keep his trap shut. He had his hands behind his back, and he twiddled his fingers nervously.

"Maybe he's stupid," said Suspenders.

Louie came right up to Jimmy, towering above him, and grinned broadly. His breath smelled like Mrs. Periwinkle's cooking. Jimmy looked down at his feet, avoiding the man's bug-eyed stare and bad breath. "Naw, he ain't stupid, Jingo. He just ain't real friendly."

Louie walked behind Jimmy and tried the barn door. It was rock solid. "Hey Jingo," he said, turning to face the other two men. "What's the international sign of friendship? Maybe he speaks Canadian. Maybe he don't understand English!" He stood in front of Jimmy and waved his arms around. "We're friends of Mr. Wagner. Do-you-know-where-he-is?"

Jimmy was beginning to wish he'd gone home for lunch. He shrugged his shoulders at the waving man.

"We," Louie pointed to himself and his men, "friends." He smiled, waving for the other men to show their teeth. The three of them stood with ape-like grins under their hats, and it was all Jimmy could do to keep from laughing. "We," he pointed again, "friends." He reached into his pocket and took out his wallet.

Louie took a green bill out of his wallet and waved it towards Jimmy. "Mr. Wagner?" he said, pointing to the house. "Where is he?" He held out the money, but Jimmy just shrugged.

"Are they all this stupid up here, Jingo? They know what *money* is don't they?" He put the money back into his wallet and turned back to Jingo and Suspenders.

"So, whadda we do now? We've tried gettin' into this barn before. We'd have to burn it down to get in there. Maybe that's what we should do. I, for one, ain't goin' back to New York with no money and no Butts Wagner, are you?" He turned back to Jimmy. The grin had been replaced by a scowl. "Where is he? Is he in the barn? Come on, kid, ya'll better start singin'."

"He don't understand, Louie. This is a waste of time." Suspenders wagged his head at Louie. "An' Wagner's here all right. He's cracked up, too, by the look of things. Look at this baseball diamond!" He slipped his thumbs under the straps at his sides and bent toward Louie. "If you men don't mind, I think we oughta call up Mr. Hogg and tell him we got a deadbeat here. We ain't gonna get any money out of Wagner. I wonder what he'll want us to do with a guy with a ten thousand dollar loan and no sign of wanting to pay it."

"I'm always glad it ain't me I come callin' on...I don't think I'd wanna be Butts Wagner just about now," snorted Jingo. He smacked Louie on the shoulder and guided him toward the corner of the barn. Jingo looked back at Jimmy and sneered.

"I know you can hear me, kid. An' I know you got a mouth as well as ears. If you've got anything between them ears, you'll listen good, and give a message to Wagner. If he ain't got one thousand dollars to put down on his loan in one week, he'd better make his funeral arrangements. I'm not called Jingo the Shooter for nothin'. I don't miss twice. You jus' deliver the message to Wagner and nobody'll get hurt... well, not till this time next week, tee hee hee," he twittered.

Jimmy watched the three of them walk slowly back to the big red car and climb in. They backed down the lane to the road and sped away in a cloud of dust. He packed up what was left of his lunch, and sat down on the home-plate bench. Where was Butts? Why did he leave him there with those gangsters? What did the guy mean by making his funeral arrangements? The questions filled his head, and he moaned out loud.

"I'm givin' you twenty-five cents and you're sittin' down here dreamin' about extra innings?" Butts' voice came from the back of the house, and it was getting closer.

Jimmy jerked his head around and saw Ol' Man Wagner standing with his hands on his hips and a twinkle in his eye. He jumped up and jogged over. "How'd you get into the house? You didn't come out of the barn!" Jimmy had been sitting right next to the side door, and he would have heard if Butts had come out of the other doors.

"An' who were those guys?" Butts was forcing himself to laugh. His small belly rolled under the gray and red baseball jersey, but his eyes told Jimmy that Butts didn't find it all so funny.

"What, those guys?" He wiggled his thumb in the direction of the road. "They're just thugs. Don't you worry about them. I've seen that Jingo before, though... Jingo is the Shooter." He squinted at Jimmy, one eye closed. "You done good, boy."

Jimmy's head was reeling. He had arrived at Ol' Man Wagner's place this morning to fix a fence, and by lunch time, he'd used a baseball glove to catch balls on a professional diamond, been quizzed by thugs, and seen Ol' Man Wagner get from the barn to the house without ever crossing the yard. And for this he would get twenty-five cents at the end of the day!

"Things sure happen fast around here," Jimmy said, mostly to himself. "So how come thugs are lookin' for you, Mr... ah, Butts? And how'd you get into the house?"

Butts laid his arm over Jimmy's shoulders. "Where there's a will, boy, there's a way. Ya know, things ain't always just the way they look. Always leave room for the improbable." He steered Jimmy back to the side door of the barn. "James Fox, one day you'll look back on today as a very important moment in your life."

"You see, this here is a dream, Jimmy. You know what it's like to have a dream?" He flipped the latch on the door and swung it back on its hinges. Jimmy knew it had been barred from the inside, and the question was dancing on his lips, but Butts kept on talking. "A dream is a message. My dream was to revolutionize baseball. And this," he swept his arm over the incredible jumble of wood, machines, and strange implements, "this is what my dream looks like."

"Those guys want me to give up." He moved through the piles of wood, rolls of cloth, crates holding unimaginable treasures and stopped in front of the gigantic machine in the middle of the room. He buffed the shiny steel rollers with his sleeve.

"Those thugs, and others like 'em, want me to wake up and stop dreaming. But I'm not just a dreamer. This isn't just a dream, James. This is as real as you and me." Ol' Man Wagner stepped to the far end of the long rolling table and pulled a red lever. The machine howled to life.

BAARRAAP! ZIGGAAP! HUNK HUNK HUNK BAAR-RAP! Its long spidery claw arms snapped and waved across the gleaming monster. Butts moved to the side of the machine and cranked first one and then another of the handles. Jimmy stood with his hands over his ears, staring at the spectacle.

"Would you say this was a dream, James?" the old man yelled over the din. He was smiling broadly now, a fresh toothpick dancing to the rhythm of the CACHUNK! OUMP, OUMP CACHUNK! OUMP, OUMP CACHUNK! of the iron-clad octopus. "*This*, my boy, will *revolutionize* baseball. This is my work of genius!"

Butts pulled the red lever back to slow down the snapping and rolling. He checked the dials at each corner and, satisfied, took a short, fat dowel made of clean white lumber and placed it into a slot at the far end. The first set of jaws snatched up the dowel and swung it slowly down to the rollers. The wood was turned around and around by the spinning silver casters.

Butts turned the cranks, and the dowel was whittled down into a perfectly shaped baseball bat. The next set of arms took up the bat and spun it around so that the butt end faced down. Butts had fed a smaller, black length of wood onto the other end of the machine. It was carved into a long spiral.

Meanwhile, the bat was disappearing slowly into a hole in the rumbling table, sending a thin white rain of wood chips all over the barn.

"This is the miracle, James, watch!" The long spiral was wound into the small hole the machine had drilled in the bat. Once it was wound in, it was handed to another pair of jaws, and placed on a large rack next to the machine. Butts pulled the red lever back and the machine sputtered into silence.

8

The Wagner Whacker

"This, my boy, is the Wagner Whacker." Butts picked the new-made bat off the rack."It's the most important thing to happen to baseball since Alexander Cartwright measured out the base lines. The Wagner Whacker is a bat designed to make baseball history. It's lightweight, virtually indestructible, and, when used correctly, will make balls go higher, faster, and, in a word, will *revolutionize* the game! And, James," Butts rubbed the bat with the palm of his hand and stared off into space, "it's only the beginning."

He hefted the bat over an imaginary home plate. "Whack!" he shouted, swinging the bat ferociously, "And that one's gone!

"The problem is that I can't make them all by myself. And I'm just about clean out of cash. Everything I saved went into buying this place and getting it ready for production." Jimmy sat down on a pile of lumber and settled in to hear the story. "Those guys, those low-life weasels, they're sent to collect on the loan for this twenty-ton manufacturing marvel. I designed it myself, and had it built by the American Manufactory and Forge of Pittsburgh, Pennsylvania. Unfortunately, I just haven't got the money. I didn't have it six months ago when the loan was due, and I haven't got it now. "

Butts put the fat end of the bat on the ground, and perched his behind on the other end, leaning on it with ease. "I've had some interest in it, and in the new baseball I've designed, too, The Wagner Spinner, I call it... but I've just plain run out of money."

"So let me get this straight," said Jimmy. He thought he understood most of the details, though it all seemed as crazy as a baseball field in the middle of nowhere. "You're going to make bats and balls for baseball teams, and you've spent all your money on getting the equipment you need to do it. And now that you have all the stuff, you can't afford to make the bats or balls?" Butts nodded. "Those guys want to take the machine away?"

Jimmy looked over the machine from one end to the other. It was the size of a hay wagon, and made of solid iron and steel. Jimmy figured it must weigh a hundred tons. "Don't worry, Butts, they'll never *move* it!" He could see that Butts didn't think it was funny. "Why don't you just tell them you'll give them the money as soon as you sell some of your bats?"

Butts wagged his head, frowning at the ground. "I wish it were that simple, James. Unfortunately, it's not. Let me size up the problem for you. You seem a smart boy, maybe you'll understand.

"In this barn is all the equipment and supplies needed to manufacture perhaps ten thousand bats, fifteen or twenty thousand balls, and four thousand of the most rugged and safe base bags ever seen. I owe ten thousand dollars, plus interest, to Mr. Ambrose Hogg of the Allegheny River Loan Company.

"Mr. Hogg is a very rich man. He's not a very nice man, but he's a very rich man. I told him I'd have a thousand dollars back to him by the end of the month, an' well, that ain't gonna happen. I don't know what's gonna happen." Butts wagged his head and spit out the toothpick. He was good with a toothpick, and could make it stick up in the dirt when he spit them out. If he stood anywhere for very long, there was always a tiny toothpick forest around his boots. This one lay flat on its side, sprawled out like a dead soldier.

Jimmy squinted out into the sunlit baseball diamond. He could see a wagon coming up the road. Butts saw it too. He put his hands in his back pockets and strutted out of the barn and up the lane to meet it.

Jimmy dragged a length of fencing lumber out to the side of the barn and watched Butts bob down the little hill to meet the wagon. He figured he should be working, but with all this excitement going on all around him, it was hard to go back to mending a broken fence. He set the wood down and looked back over to the road. He didn't care about the twenty-five cents anymore, he had to know what was going to happen next.

He crossed over to the outhouse, and from there crept along the side of the main house to the orchard, where he watched Butts wait for the wagon to arrive. It was only Mr. Broad. Mr. Broad lived on the next concession and sometimes brought the mail by Jimmy's house when he'd been in town. He had a letter for Butts.

Jimmy watched as Ol' Man Wagner waved his neighbor on his way. He lay hidden in the tall grass behind a stump and watched the old man tear open the letter. He wondered what Mr. Broad thought when he saw Butts all dressed up for a big game. By now, nothing about Butts Wagner surprised Jimmy.

Butts dropped the hand holding the letter to his side and put the other hand on his hip. Then he held up the letter again and slowly shook his head. "James!" he said, looking into the thick orchard to find Jimmy's tiny face among the branches. "Come on outta there, boy!" He stared directly into Jimmy's eyes.

Jimmy stood up and wiped himself off. He couldn't figure how Butts knew he was there. He hadn't made a sound, and he hadn't moved... How could Butts see him? He scrambled to his feet.

"When are you gonna be through with that fence, boy, *Saturday?*"

The old man marched back to his barn, swinging his arms and wagging his head. Jimmy rubbed the grassy itch out of his arms and followed the man with his flapping letter back to the baseball diamond. Butts turned at home plate and disappeared into the barn. Jimmy caught up in time to see Ol' Man Wagner floating up to his cozy home in the rafters.

He was determined to find out more about the Wagner Baseball Equipment Company and the Wagner Whacker. Jimmy decided it was more important than fixing the fence, so he grabbed the first rung of the long ladder and swung into action. Hand over hand he climbed higher and higher above the bat machine and the rows of boxes, lumber piles and work tables. Looking down was making him dizzy, so Jimmy fixed his eyes on the trap door above. "Mr. Wagner?" he called, "Butts?"

For a moment, nobody answered, but soon he heard boots on the platform in front of him. Then the latch snapped, the door swung up, and Butts' head appeared in the opening. "Watch that next rung, James, it's a bit tricky. I'm gonna fix it one day."

"Come on in, James. There's an easier way, ya know. Just whistle from below. I'll ride down an' get ya next time."

Jimmy sat his rear end up on the platform, and Butts closed the hatch in his living room floor. "I was just thinkin' Butts," There was something Jimmy didn't understand. Ol' Man Wagner had all the lumber, the machine, pots and pots of varnish and paint, and everything was in place to make the bats. So why didn't he just get busy making bats instead of building a baseball diamond in the middle of the night?

"I was just wondering if we shouldn't be making bats instead of fixing fences..."

Butts swooped up a toothpick from a little cup in the middle of the table, and stretched out his legs. He snorted and leaned back into his chair. "You know who this letter is from?" Jimmy shook his head. "It's from the greatest baseball player in the world. It's from my kid brother." He handed Jimmy the envelope, made out to The Wagner Baseball Equipment Company, Albertus Wagner, Proprietor.

"The letter is from Honus. He says 'Butts; Hope this letter finds you in good spirits. Have some news about your bats. It's all arranged that if you want to bring some down for a tryout, the Pirates are willing to give them a go at the exhibition game in Watertown on Sunday, June 3 at one p.m. See you then,' and it's signed 'Honus'. So what d'ya think of that?"

"That's what I've been sayin', Butts, we should be makin' baseball bats!" Jimmy saw Butts' worried face curl up into a smile.

"James, I'd have to have six good pairs of hands at the machine, twelve hours a day for the next five days, and I ain't got a plug nickel to pay those hands, even if I could find 'em. To top it off, nearly everybody from Fergus to Markdale thinks I'm some sort of cranky Yankee, and wouldn't give me the time of day, much less do a day's work for a thank-you-kindly!" The toothpick spun furiously.

"I just can't do it all myself. I've got the bases loaded, two out, and a full count. What I need is a pinch hitter who can put the ball over the fence. But the bench is empty, and I'm not sure I can plug me a homer anymore..."

Jimmy scratched his head at all this baseball talk. He tried to think of something to say that would help, but he couldn't think of anything that sounded any good. He already offered to help run the machine, and that was all he could think of. "Why don't we just start making a few and we can take them to wherever this Watertown is?"

"Oh, we could make a dozen a day, you and I. But with a full crew this machine'll zip off fifty or sixty bats a day, depending on the specifications for the bats.

"The Pittsburgh Pirates are one of the finest teams in the game. Pittsburgh is known for ingenuity, but also for careful calculation. I'm only gonna get one tryout. If they like 'em, they'll order enough Wagner Whackers to begin full production. If they don't, it'll be a cold August in Poughkeepsie before they agree to try 'em again.

"The Wagner Whacker is not just a baseball bat, James, it's a baseball bat *system*. You've got your long-ball bats, your bunting bats, you're right-hander-left-field bats, your left-hand-line-dri-vers... It's a system. Each bat has been carefully planned, with scientific principles, determining the weight, length, and grip of each sort of bat. A basic set would include more than a hundred different bats."

"A hundred!" Jimmy yelled. "A hundred bats for nine guys? What d'ya need a hundred bats for?"

"Just a minute," Butts said, rummaging around on his book-shelf. He took a piece of paper out from the pages of a thick brown book and added up numbers in his head. "To go to

Watertown, New York and show 'em what the Wagner Whacker can do on the field, I'd have to have 132 bats in the set, and it's only fair that each team be given a set, so as to even up the odds. That's 264 bats, James.

"I'd need six men on the machine for, oh, a week or so. Then they have to be sanded, polished and varnished to perfection, and tested, too... Heavy bats, light bats, wide grips, narrow grips, various balance points and sweet spots... it's very exacting, boy.

"So the long and the short of it is that it's impossible to get 264 bats to Watertown a week from Sunday morning. And if I don't get 264 bats to Watertown, I don't know what'll happen. It's what you call a conundrum." Jimmy didn't know what a conundrum was, but he figured it was bad.

"So what do we do now?" Jimmy felt completely confused and helpless. "Are we gonna just sit here?" He knew they should be doing something.

"What are we gonna do?" the old man echoed. He sauntered over to the elevator and nodded Jimmy aboard. He was silent until the flying pallet touched down on the barn floor. "What we're gonna do is this: you're gonna work on that fence and I'm gonna sit and ponder over how to make a silk purse out of a sow's ear. Maybe I can get a few winks and figure out how the dream is supposed to end."

The machine lurched upward and Jimmy was left among the piles of wood, and boxes marked 'Wagner Baseball Equipment Company, Fergus, Ontario.'

9

You Wouldn't Believe Me If I Told You...

When the sun had crossed over the best part of the day, Jimmy packed up Ol' Man Wagner's toolbox, and called up into the barn. "Mr. Wagner! Butts! I'm done!" he yelled, and waited for some sign of the old man. After about five minutes he called again, with the same silent result. "Are you up there, Mr. Wagner? I've got to get home for my supper." He felt stupid talking to himself, so he just shrugged his shoulders and headed for home.

Once he'd washed and changed his clothes, he plopped down on his bed, waiting for his mom to call him for dinner. Hal came in and shuffled around in his cupboard.

"Hey, Jimmy, what'd you do at Ol' Man Wagner's place? Is he real mean?" Jimmy didn't know where to start, and Hal's questions kept on coming. "Have you seen my jacks? Did you know King got into trouble diggin' in the flower beds? Is Ol' Man Wagner a Yankee bank robber?"

Jimmy was half listening and half thinking about the amazing things he'd seen today. "You wouldn't believe me if I told you Hal."

"Jimmy! Hal! Supper! It's on the table, so don't dawdle!" They were both up in a flash and elbowed each other for headway along the hall, fought for first place down the stairs, and finally Hal made a big finish, ducking under Jimmy's arm at the dining room door.

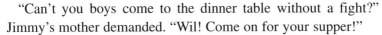

"Can't you boys come to the dinner table without a fight?" Jimmy's mother demanded. "Wil! Come on for your supper!"

The boys took their places at the table and began ladling food onto their plates. They had roast chicken, potatoes, dumplings, carrots, beets and gravy. It was all too hot to eat, but they weren't allowed to dig in until their father sat down anyway.

Wil Fox came in and sat at the head of the table, bowed his head and mumbled grace. When his head came up, the clattering of spoons, forks and china began. Hal ate like he'd never seen food before, but Jimmy was keeping up shovelful for shovelful.

Mr. Fox turned to Jimmy, pointing with his fork. "Slow down, son, there's plenty for all of us. What did you do for Mr. Wagner today? Is he keepin' you out of trouble? I don't suppose you've had much time for fiddling around, eh? Planting more potatoes today?"

Jimmy looked over at Hal's plate, then at the pan of chicken in the middle of the table, and he figured he could afford the time out to talk. Hal had a ways to go before he could reach over for the last leg, and if he hurried, he could get to it first.

"Well, this morning," he said in a rush, "I played outfield. With a glove. Behind second base. And I caught all the balls, and then I was fixing the fence, and three thugs came in a big red car, and Butts locked the barn from the inside, and I didn't say anything to the thugs, and then Mr. Wagner came out of the house, when he never left the barn. That was after the three men left, and then Butts made a bat on his machine that will revolute baseball, and then..."

"Wait a minute! Hold on, one thing at a time. You played baseball? With who?" His dad was smiling a what-an-imagination smile. "Where were you playing baseball?"

"On the field. It's the best darn baseball field in the known world." He caught his mother frowning at the 'darn' part. "Sorry, Mom. Mr. Wagner built a baseball diamond. It has white lines all over and brand new white bases, and a hill for the pitcher and everything. Butts, Mr. Wagner, isn't a bank robber. He's a baseball player! His brother plays for the Pittsburgh Pirates Baseball Club, and he's the best ballplayer who ever lived. Butts taught him everything he knows." Jimmy felt pretty important. He liked saying Butts, when he should be saying Mr. Wagner.

"Mr. Wagner is a baseball player?" Jimmy's dad was suddenly very interested. His mom was pinching up her face, trying to make sense of what Jimmy was talking about. Hal had stopped eating. He sat with his eyes switching from his father to Jimmy and back again.

"Yes sir. He played for the Brooklyn Dodgers, and the Washington Senators. He's got the uniform and everything. And he built a whole baseball field last night." Suddenly Jimmy realized how unbelievable all this must be.

"Mr. Wagner's brother plays for the Pittsburgh Pirates? Honus Wagner? Irma, did you know Ol' Man Wagner was Honus Wagner's brother?"

"I don't even know who Honus Wagner is! How would I know Mr. Wagner was a baseball player?" Irma protested. Hal's head swung from his mother back to his father, and he poured a fresh glass of milk.

"Honus Wagner is probably the best baseball player who ever lived. He's retired these days, but if I were a gambling man, I'd wager he'd still be the best man on the field." Wil turned back to Jimmy. "And Ol' Man Wagner is Honus Wagner's brother. Well ain't that somethin'."

Jimmy couldn't believe that his father knew about Honus Wagner. He hadn't completely believed Butts about the Pittsburgh Pirates and the Washington Senators, but he did now. "And he's going to make baseball bats and balls with his machines, only the thugs don't want him to, because he owes them money, and the one called Jingo is The Shooter."

"Slow down, again, Jimmy Fox," Irma piped in. "What about these thugs? Are you making all this up? Because if you are..."

"No. I swear it. I mean, sorry, Mom." He wasn't supposed to swear, and that was the second time he'd done it in five minutes. "They had a huge red car. A Cadillac, and they were from the States, and they thought I didn't understand English. They were looking for Butts, but he locked himself in the barn, and I didn't say nothin' to them, and when they left, Mr. Wagner came out of the house!"

Jimmy forked back some more chicken, and between mouthfuls told the whole story of the day's events.

"Well that's quite a tale, son. I guess you've had a day you'll remember." Wil sat back in his chair as Irma refilled his coffee mug. "I suppose you've got another day at the Wagner place in mind, eh?"

"You bet! I ain't even got my twenty-five cents for today! I gotta go back tomorrow first thing. Butts is gonna give me Lesson Number Three. And we've gotta figure out how to make all those bats! And I ain't even seen the ball making machine yet. You should see the elevator up to his house!" Hal was hanging on every word, eyes wide, and more than a little jealous.

"I think we'll all head over to see Mr. Wagner in the morning. I want to see this baseball diamond!" Wil Fox stretched his legs out under the table and pulled at his chin. He was picturing what he'd say to the cranky older brother of the greatest ballplayer who ever lived. Wil wasn't really a baseball man, but he'd sure heard of Honus Wagner.

"I want to know about the thugs who come around in a big red automobile from the United States," said Jimmy's worried mother. "I want to know what's going on a hundred yards from my back door!"

"I just want to ride on the elevator!" Hal burst in. "And I'll bet there's a secret door to the house!" he laughed.

10

Six Good Men

The early morning sun saw the entire Fox family trudging across their field towards the Wagner place. Hal, Jimmy and King ran ahead, followed closely by Wil and Irma. "I want to know there's not going to be any trouble out here with Jimmy around, Wil. You make sure there's not going to be any trouble."

"We'll get to the bottom of this, Irma. I don't think we've got too much to worry about. You know how these boys like to exaggerate." As they approached the newly mended fence, Wil stopped short. Ol' Man Wagner was kneeling in the short grass out behind second base, in the middle of a baseball field.

"Irma, do you see what I think I see?" The two of them stood side by side with their mouths open.

Mr. Wagner was crawling backwards, painting white lines in the outfield grass. Each base was surrounded by large squares of brown dirt, and crisp white lines extended from each square to the next. Beyond the clean white bags was a series of smaller white lines extending in both directions, making a checkerboard of large green squares in the outfield. Each of the squares had a number painted in the middle. They stood and watched Mr. Wagner paint J-11 into a square.

Irma went white. She was too stunned to speak; she just stood with her hand over her mouth. Some of the neighbors had said Mr. Wagner was a bit crazy, and now she was sure it was true. She

72

liked to think the best of people, but this was too much. He must be as mad as a hatter. Why else would a grown man waste his time painting lines in the grass? "William, for heaven's sake, what is he doing out there?"

"I haven't the slightest idea." Wil was wondering the same thing. "Whatever it is, I've got a feeling Jimmy hasn't told us the half of it."

"G'mornin' James. Who's this, now?" Butts called as Jimmy and Hal came running up. "I've gotta give you each a quarter today?"

Hal nearly wet his pants at the mention of twenty-five cents. "I'm Hal," he blurted.

"I'm Butts. Glad to know you Harold." The old man reached out his hand and pumped the surprised youngster's arm.

"If you're here to work, I think I can find somethin' to keep ya busy. Are ya as talkative as your brother, boy?" Hal was still too amazed at the idea of earning money to answer questions himself.

"What are you doin' out here? What is this? Jimmy says you've got a machine to make baseball bats, and an elevator and that it's all a dream. Do ya think I could ride the elevator? And how d'you get into the barn from the house? And are you really the greatest baseball player who ever lived?"

Butts squinted over at Jimmy. "Kinda quiet, ain't he, James. Doesn't he ever ask any questions?" Butts laughed and dusted off his knees. "I ain't the best baseball player in the world. Heck, I'm probably not even second best," he laughed.

"You look like a second base man to me. I'll bet you play second base, don'cha?" he grinned.

"He ain't ever played any base. Hal couldn't hit a sleeping dog with a broom," Jimmy piped up.

"Is that your mother and dad comin' across the field, Harold?" Butts could see them standing frozen in the pasture. "The whole *skulk* of Foxes, eh, boys?" He looked over to Jimmy and winked. "I'm just glad I ain't a goose with all these foxes in the field!

"G'mornin, Mrs. Fox, Mr. Fox. Fine morning," he called. Butts looked completely composed. He seemed unaware of how strange he must look dressed in a baseball uniform, strutting across a checkerboard baseball diamond at seven o'clock in the morning with his arm extended for a neighborly handshake.

"I don't mean to be rude, Mr. Wagner, but what are you doing?" said Jimmy's father. "Jimmy told us you had some peculiar ways, but..." he stammered, "...this is a baseball field!"

"I can imagine how it looks, Mr. Fox, but I assure you, it's all perfectly scientific. Yes, it is a baseball diamond all right. In fact," he said, removing the toothpick from his lips, "it's the *perfect baseball diamond*. The Good Lord made this piece of ground to be a baseball field, ma'am. That's what I need to make perfect baseball equipment, the perfect baseball field."

Irma was almost in shock. Her neighbor, wearing a peculiar uniform, had planted a baseball diamond in his best field, and was telling her that the Good Lord had planned things that way. Her lips trembled and her hands were clutched tightly at her sides. Wagner didn't seem to notice. He continued explaining the situation in the same calm tone.

"You see, to accurately design the perfect baseball equipment, it is necessary to test it on a field which is absolutely exact in it's measurements and response. I know how to build the equipment, and very soon, I'll have the ground to test it on."

Wil was overwhelmed by the bizarre, but confident explanation. For a minute, he didn't think all this was so strange after all.

Irma saw her husband nodding in agreement, but she wasn't convinced by the story. She bit her lip, and said sternly, "Jimmy says there was some trouble over here yesterday. Some men in a big red car threatening him. I don't want him mixed up in anything, Mr. Wagner — do we Wil?"

"Oh, them. Don't you worry about them, ma'am. I'm not worried about them." Butts was worried about Hogg's men. He didn't think Jimmy was in any danger though.

"Why don't we all go on up an' have a cup of coffee. I think I can set your mind at ease, Mrs. Fox. Come on up for a cup of hot coffee." And with that, he led the whole Fox family along to home plate.

"Welcome," said Wagner as they entered the cool, woody-smelling barn, "to the Wagner Baseball Equipment Company!"

Wil Fox whistled at the huge bat-making machine. "Lord above us, Mr. Wagner, whatever is this?"

"This, Mr. Fox, is the future of baseball." Butts stood proudly beside his monstrous invention. "There's only one of these, and this is it. This is the machine to revolutionize the greatest game ever invented." He rubbed a white cloth over the silver rollers and polished up the glass dials on the side. "This is a baseball dream machine. With it, I can make baseball bats to the most exacting standards ever imagined. Think of it, Mr. Fox, Mrs. Fox. Baseball is a hitting game. The bat is the hitting instrument." Butts leaned back on the machine, and fixed his eyes on them.

"Like any instrument, it should fit the person using it. In this case, that's the batter." He popped a slim toothpick into his mouth and looked over at Mrs. Fox, nodding. "Some men have bigger hands, stronger wrists, weaker shoulders, and so on. So the weight of the bat needs to be adjusted to the way the player swings naturally. Do you follow?"

Irma was amazed that it all made sense, but it did. She nodded for him to continue, which was all the encouragement he needed.

"So the weight of the bat can be sort of moved around. We can adjust the machine to make it lighter at the fat end, or more toward the middle. That way a hitter with strong hands but weak shoulders can swing the bat around as fast as a more powerfully built man. We can put a thirty-three-ounce bat, which is very heavy for a baseball bat, into the hands of a weak hitter, and he can swing it with the ease of a giant.

"So you see, Mrs. Fox, baseball players come in different sizes, so why shouldn't the bats they use come in different sizes? And," Butts turned to Wil, "different game situations call for different types of approach. Sometimes you want a home run bat, but counting on the long ball is always a risk. You never know what kind of air currents or scuffs on the ball will keep Doctor Long-Ball from delivering a screaming home run, no matter how hard he spanks it. So sometimes what you want is a flair-out behind second base. To get a different sort of hit, you use a different bat. My diamond will be used to test the different weights, types of wood, and lengths of bats to hit a fastball into different places on the field. That's why I've been painting the graph out there in the outfield. I've got records and charts for every big league park in the eastern circuit, so I know just what I'm up against."

"You mean all those squares out there... You're building a base-ball equipment factory?" Wil asked, hardly believing his own eyes and ears. Was it possible that Mr. Wagner wasn't crazy at all? That this all made as much sense as he seemed to believe it did? "I thought for a moment..." He didn't finish the sentence, but let it hang in the air.

"Come on upstairs, folks. We'll have a cup of coffee and I'll show you how it all works." Butts stepped over to the elevator and cranked on the motor. Hal didn't miss a beat, and was standing next to him before you could say Jack the Bear. Jimmy wasn't far behind, thinking how unbelievable it was that his mother and father were actually going to see Butts's home in the rafters.

"Come on, Mrs. Fox, it's perfectly safe. Just hang on to the rail, and don't look down." Wil looked up to the rafters doubtfully. The ropes were sturdy. The pulleys seemed to be secured in the beams. He looked at the long ladder up against the wall of the barn, and considered the climb.

He helped his wife aboard and stepped up onto the platform behind her. She wasn't too sure of the contraption, but she was willing to trust her husband's judgement. Butts jerked the motor into action and continued his tale as they rose above the dirt floor, above the crates and stacks of wood and into the upper reaches of the building. "I've brought heavier loads up here, folks, just relax and enjoy it. It's a whole lot easier than the stairs," he chuckled, pointing to the ladder.

The elevator came to a stop alongside the loft, and they were all very glad to step onto the safety of the loft floor. Butts had cof-fee on the burner and poured some out for the adults. He yanked two soda pops out of a cold bucket of water for the boys, smiling at Hal.

"Where I come from, kids just love soda for breakfast!" Hal had never had soda pop before. He turned it slowly in his fingers, his eyes drinking up the idea of having this for breakfast every morning. Jimmy pried his bottle open with Mr. Wagner's jack-knife, which he now kept regularly in his back pocket, and reached over to help his brother. "Where'd ya get that?" Hal whistled, his eyes popping and his hands reaching to take the knife from Jimmy.

"It belongs to Butts," said Jimmy, letting his brother look the knife over.

"I'd like you to see this, Mrs. Fox. Have a look at this view." Irma Fox had never been anywhere near this high off the ground. She stood marvelling over the expanse of country in front of her.

"Oh, my... This is really wonderful. Wil, Hal, you won't believe how pretty our farm is from up here." She watched her clean white washing blowing in the breeze below, and the acres of green fields rolling off into the distance. Butts pointed out the straight lines in Jimmy's potato patch, and complimented her on his fine work. "The boy's a good worker, Mrs. Fox. And well mannered, too," he said.

Irma was still in awe of the idea of Wagner living up in the loft. "I don't wonder why you live up here, Mr. Wagner. I think I could even get used to that machine just to wake up to this view every morning."

"Yes, Mrs. Fox. My thoughts exactly. After living up here I don't think I could ever get used to living so low to the ground again."

She leaned up against the window and studied the horizon, as the others settled around the table or on the sofa. Joining them at the table, she blew the steam off her coffee and sipped the hot black drink.

Butts' eyes scanned the room and he smiled, proud to finally have visitors. "It's always been my dream that one day I could put all I've learned about baseball to some good use. I've spent my life watching people play ball. Boys, men, hackers, pros, girls, women, black men, yellow men, red men; I think I've seen more baseball than any man alive. And now, I want to share some of what I've learned.

"These bats will revolutionize the game. They'll move back the fences, even build new parks, if they have to. The game will evolve. The record book will have two sections: pre-Wagner and post-Wagner. And the bats are just the beginning." Butts' voice trailed off. Then he seemed to snap back and he grinned at everybody. "It's a dream. I know, it's a big dream, but what's the point of a small one?"

"You see, Mr. Fox, as I told your James, I have nearly everything in place, but there's one thing I hadn't counted on. It's the men, you see." They didn't see. They looked at him, waiting for him to explain.

"I've got everything I need right here except the men. I need six workmen to help me make the dream come true. They'd have to learn quick, and believe that they can make the finest baseball equipment ever whittled, painted or sewn. I think I could find six such workmen here in Fergus, but the well has run dry. I've just run clean out of money. One day, this company may employ as many young men as Fergus can produce, but right now, I don't think I could find men to work for what I could offer them, which is nothin'."

Butts poured a second cup of coffee for himself, and held up the pot to refill Wil and Irma's mugs. "You see, there's a solution to this, I just haven't found it yet. My best ideas come to me while I'm asleep, and I've been too busy to put in much time on the ol' bunk lately. But I'm not worried. I've got a strong feeling that the solution will present itself, and I'll know it when I see it."

Irma moved back to the bank of windows and quietly listened to the conversation. Wil was asking about the cost of bats, and how many Wagner thought he could sell, and how long it would take to make them, and he seemed truly amazed at the amount of detail Wagner had at the tip of his tongue.

Even she could tell that although Butts Wagner was more than a little peculiar, he knew what he was talking about. He just wasn't very practical. She stepped over to the rail and studied the silent equipment on the barn floor, imagining a dozen workers grinding bats and unloading crates.

Suddenly, something occurred to her. A secret smile came to

her lips as the picture of workers on the floor became clearer in her mind. Wagner's dream didn't have to be just a dream. He just needed to think more practically.

"Mr. Wagner," Irma Fox said quietly.

"Yes, Mrs. Fox? And please, call me Butts. My Christian name is Albertus, but I've been called Butts since I was a boy in short pants."

"All right... Butts," she said, "I just wonder... You said you needed six men to make your dream come true. In my experience, men have never been much good at dreams." She swept her strawberry hair back over her forehead. "I'm not sure what sort of men you need, but I just wonder if those men might be *women*?"

11

Cleats

Butts stared at her, bewildered. He shook his head as if he hadn't heard her correctly. She smiled back at him and sipped at her mug. He slipped a toothpick into his mouth and spun it around furiously. A smile was forming at the corners of his mouth, but it was taking its time. He glanced at Jimmy and Hal on the sofa, then back to Irma. The grin was not yet in full bloom, but she could see that he was considering the strange idea she had suggested.

"Like I said, Mr. Fox," said Wagner, the smile on his face now stretching from ear to ear, "when the answer presents itself, I'll be ready to recognize it."

He looked Irma straight in the eye as she approached the table. He had no doubt that she had more to say on the subject, and he was eager to hear it. "I've always been of the belief that women and men are exactly the same," Ol' Man Wagner sipped his coffee and waited for her to sit at the table across from him, "except that women are smarter...

"You have something in mind, Mrs. Fox?"

"I might, Mr. Wagner." Irma pushed her cup forward, accepting the coffee Wagner was silently offering her. "I know some women around here... some very able women, Mr. Wagner."

Wil said nothing. He recognized his wife's 'organize the church picnic' voice.

"The women I know haven't just made dreams happen, Mr. Wagner, I've seen some miracles brought to life around here. What do you need these men to do?"

"Well, it's not too complicated, but it's dirty work, and loud." Butts turned to Jimmy. "You'd say it was loud wouldn'tcha, James?" He smiled back at Irma, and winked at Hal, who was sucking the last drips from his soda pop bottle. "But you must understand, Mrs. Fox, I can't afford to pay anybody."

"I understand that, Mr. Wagner, but I also understand something about neighborliness. You may be a newcomer here, and you've got your strange ways, but you are, after all, a neighbor. If it were a new barn you needed, or a sickness in your home, we'd be here to do what's right." Wil was smiling proudly and shaking his head. Irma put her hands face down on the table and looked directly across at Butts. "You'll have your turn, Mr. Wagner. We give, and we receive..."

"A generous offer, Mrs. Fox. But I just couldn't accept it. If anyone's gonna work in my factory, they're gonna be paid for it." He rocked back in his chair and drummed his fingers on the table. His eyes rolled up in his head, and except for the drumming of his fingers, he seemed for all the world to be fast asleep. He sat for a long minute while the Fox family looked uncomfortably at one another. Finally, he spoke.

"I can do two things. First, I can offer you men's wages, to be paid, with interest, when the money comes in, and second," he swirled his toothpick around his mouth, thinking of exactly how to say what he had in mind, "and second, I think I can arrange to have the Pittsburgh Pirates Baseball Club pay a visit to Fergus... picnic baskets and lazy fly balls... what baseball was meant to be... A summertime demonstration of the greatest game ever invented."

"Mom! A real baseball team in Fergus!" Jimmy jumped off the couch and stood, eyes blazing, between his mother and father. "A real baseball team, right here? They can play on the diamond!"

"Mr. Wagner, I do believe you've got yourself a deal," said Wil. "Irma, who exactly have you got in mind?"

"Wil, you just leave this to me. I don't think I'll have any trouble finding a team for Mr. Wagner's baseball factory. You just hitch up the buggy and wish me luck." She rose from her chair and walked to the rail at the edge of the platform.

Butts stood up and looked over at Hal. He was staring at the bucket of water, wondering if there was any more soda in there. The old man rolled up his sleeve and dipped into the water, coming up with three wet bottles, which he set on the table. He nodded to Jimmy, who sprang over to open them, as Butts bent to pull out two more brown bottles, wiping them on the leg of his pants. "Mrs. Fox, I think this calls for a little celebration. Boys, Mr. Fox," he said, passing the open bottles of soda pop all around.

"Here's to the superior mind of the female race!" Butts chirped, clinking his bottle against Hal's. They all clinked bottles and gulped the sweet fizzy syrup.

"Here's to the Wagner Baseball Equipment Company!" laughed Irma. She clinked her bottle against Wagner's, "And Butts," she said, looking from him to Wil and back, "call me Irma!"

B ack at home Jimmy and Hal helped their father hitch up the horse and buggy. Irma climbed aboard and clattered off down the lane. "Well, boys," said Wil as he watched his wife roll away, "I don't know exactly what she's got cooked up, but I think Ol' Man Wagner's in good hands. I don't know anybody better at solving problems than your mother, God bless her." He wiped his hands on his pants, then shaded his eyes as he looked down the lane. "Why don't you boys get back over to Mr. Wagner's place and see if he needs your help this morning? I've got some chores right here, but I'll mosey back over later on."

"Jimmy," Hal asked as the two boys and the dog were crossing the field, "do ya think I could play second base?"

"If Butts says you're a second baseman, I'd be willing to bet you could play second base. Baseball is his *life*." Jimmy was getting in the habit of saying just what he heard Ol' Man Wagner say. "I think we better keep our minds on work, though. If Butts wants to play baseball, he'll tell us. He don't mind sayin' what he thinks. Just don't you go askin' him for twenty-five cents. I don't think he's got too many quarters to spread around."

"And what about the Pittsburgh Pirates? Do you think he's gonna bring them to Fergus?" Hal asked.

"If Butts says he's gonna bring the finest derned baseball team in the world to Fergus, I guess he will," he said, imitating the old man's American twang.

Hal continued, "What d'ya think Ma's gonna do? D'ya think she's gonna get him some money?"

"Search me, Hal. If Pa don't know, how d'ya expect me to know? I think we're just lucky Pa didn't ask us to help *him*. Butts don't hang around tellin' ya how to do everything. 'Course, he'll probably have to tell you how to do stuff. Anyway, I don't know what he wants us to do today. Probably something scientific..."

"Hiya, boys," Butts called from inside the barn. Butts was nowhere to be seen, but the boys could hear him whistling and humming. He was somewhere back in the rows of lumber and boxes stacked neatly across the wide dirt floor.

Suddenly a bright green shirt shot up over the boxes. It was followed by a baseball glove, a pair of pants, a red shirt, a large white cloth and a small black bag. They darted through the maze of crates, and around the third row they came upon the back of his pants.

Butts Wagner was bent over at the waist, rooting through a large, low crate. The back of his trousers wobbled this way and that as he muttered and hummed, tossing things into piles on the ground around him.

"I know I've got some here... You said nine, didn't you, James?"

Hal looked at Jimmy and Jimmy looked at Butts' behind. "Nine what?" He didn't know what the old man was talking about.

"How's nine-and-a-half?" He seemed to be talking more to himself than to anybody else.

"Nine-and-a-half what?" Jimmy was getting frustrated.

"Cleats, boy. Cleats. I've got a pair of nine-and-a-half in here... Ya know, there's a future in cleats. A man could do well making cleats. There's a future in baseball, ya know." Hal and Jimmy looked at each other blankly and shrugged their shoulders. Neither of them knew what cleats were.

"What's cleats?" Hal sputtered, snickering at the legs and rear end bouncing in front of him.

"Cleats? What's cleats?" The legs shook with laughter. "Tell him, James."

"How do I know what cleats is?" said Jimmy, turning to Hal. "They're nine-and-a-half."

"*Cleats!*" Butts called. "Spikes!" He laughed, reaching deeper into the box. "*These*, my boys, are cleats!" He spun around holding out a dirty pair of black and white shoes with short nails sticking out of the bottom. "Try 'em on, James."

"Why do the shoes have teeth?" Hal asked, holding the left shoe spike side up.

"They're cleats, boy." He wagged his head at Hal, and took the shoe from his stubby little hands. "These are shoes for *runnin'*. Running shoes. These here cleats are the mark of the modern baseball player."

He handed the shoe to Jimmy, who had already laced up the right one. "Why, a man can run almost twice as fast in these shoes, and he can stop on a dime. Mark my words, Harold, one day there won't be a man on the field not wearin' cleats."

Butts got his dreamy look again, and spun his toothpick around madly. "I don't know why I didn't think of it before, but I can't see any reason we shouldn't start up a line of cleats right here. What d'ya think, boys?"

Jimmy was stomping his feet, feeling the sharp pins cut up the hard dirt of the barn floor. "Yes sir! I think we oughtta start a line of cleats," Jimmy said, smiling at Hal. He was thinking that his kid brother must be pretty jealous of these running shoes, and he was dying to try them out on the thick grass outside.

"Harold, try on this here jersey." Butts smiled, handing the young boy a very large red and blue shirt. "We can just tuck it in here and there. This jersey belonged to Whitey Lumbart, the best second baseman I ever knew, and one heck of a nice fellow. A man could do worse than wear his sweater."

Hal had the sweater over his head and tucked in at the front
before he had time to ask who Whitey Lumbart was. Jimmy was
running down the narrow row, leaving a track of small holes and
small chips of hard packed dirt behind him.

"Can I play second base, Mr. Wagner? Are we gonna have
Lesson Number Three? I haven't even had Lesson Number One!
Jimmy says you can hit the weather vane on the top of the barn!"
Hal was panting to keep up with Butts, trotting out on to the field
behind him.

"Sure I can hit the weather vane, son. Here, let's try it the *hard*
way." He was bent over again, this time poking around in a large
blue bag near home plate. He slung a bat over his shoulder, and
tossed Hal a brown leather glove and a gray baseball. Hal put the
glove on his hand and looked up to see Butts nodding. "Are you
a lefty, Harold?"

Hal didn't know what Butts was talking about. He shrugged
and watched his brother tearing around the field. "Well, are you
a lefty? I mean are you *left-handed*!" The old man shook his
head, and muttered to Hal. "You boys have got a lot to learn about
baseball. Just put the glove on your other hand, Harold. Now, toss
me the ball."

Hal gripped the ball in his small fingers and swung his arm
back over his head, and whipped it at the old man.

"Atta boy!" Butts shouted. He kept his eye closely on the spinning
leather ball, and swung the long bat. The bat came around, smacked
the ball, and sent it high up in the direction of the barn. The ball
arched just as it passed the weather vane and bonged the iron rooster, sending it twirling madly in the still air. Jimmy ran to where the
ball was rolling off the roof, and waited to catch the rebound.

The ball, of course, sailed out halfway to third base. Jimmy
backpedalled in his new spikes. "I've got it! I've got it!" he shouted.

He only got the tips of his fingers on the floating ball, but was
able to pull it into the palm of his hand and smother it against his
body before tumbling into the dirt. "I got it!" he cried.

"Nice catch, James!" Butts laughed. "Nice catch. That's what you
call a can o' corn... It's like catchin' a can o' corn fallin' off a shelf!"

"How'd you do that! You plumb *spun the rooster*!" barked Hal in surprise.

"It's the Wagner Whacker, Harold! This here's a fly-ball bat. It's long, and slender, and it's made from young ironwood. I call it a fungo bat. It's got a lot of spring, but not so much distance. It hits 'em high, but not far. And that rooster, why I was tryin' to wake *him* up for a change!"

The boys didn't do any work that sunny day, and neither did Wil Fox. He arrived in time for batting practice, and the four of them spent the entire day smacking and chasing balls around the field. With a bit of work, Ol' Man Wagner had the three of them playing like sandlot heroes, hitting, running and snagging long line drives.

12

The 24th of May

When Jimmy awoke the following morning, the sun was barely up over the flat lands to the east. He heard dishes clacking below him in the kitchen, and he had the bitter smell of fresh coffee in his nose.

"Hal!" he whispered. "It's morning. Wake up!" That was all it took to raise the sleeping pipsqueak from his dreams of baseball and soda pop. "I'm hungry!" he chirped.

Hal sat up and looked out the window next to his bed. "Hey, it must be real early. The sky's all red, an' the trees are real yellowish." He was listening to the clatter coming from downstairs. "Mom's up already. I bet she's got fried chicken for lunch. And dill pickles, and..." He stuck his head out the window, trying to look around the corner of the house to see the Wagner place. He whispered over to Jimmy, "D'ya think Butts has got any more of that soda pop?" He thought about that first fizz, when Jimmy cranked the top off the cold bottle, and added, "How come you get to have Butts's knife? Do ya think he's got another one?"

"You don't need a jackknife, Hal. You're a second baseman. Second basemen don't *need* jackknives! And how can you be thinkin' about lunch when you ain't even had *breakfast* yet?" Hal lay back down and pulled his blanket over his head. Jimmy pulled his shoes on and headed down to the outhouse. He wasn't thinking about soda pop just then. He was thinking about what was going to happen today.

When Jimmy had finished in the outhouse, he came and stood in the kitchen doorway, watching his mother pack a huge picnic basket with jars and small pots of food. She hadn't seen him come into the kitchen, and she was absent-mindedly talking to herself.

"Jean will bring enough of her strawberry jam to float a barge in, and Mrs. Periwinkle will probably bring her put-up fish." She leaned on the top of the bulging picnic basket, grunting, trying to fasten the latch. "And oh, Pip Van Broten will have a crock of her sauerkraut. Lord, how I hate Pip Van Broten's sauerkraut!"

"I ain't so fond of it either, Mom," Jimmy giggled. She spun around to find him leaning against the door jamb, with his hands in his pockets.

"Why Jimmy Fox, what makes you think you can sneak up on me like that? I ought to tan your hide!" She was sort of laughing, but her cheeks were getting pretty red, and if it was any other sort of day, she just might have been angry at his sneaking up. Today, she was too excited to get mad.

He plunked down at the kitchen table and poured a glass of fresh milk from the pitcher. His mother took the coffee pot from the stove and brought two cups to the table. "Don't you know what day it is today?" she said, setting down the cups and the pot. "Today is the 24th of May, 1928, and you're thirteen years old this morning."

He hadn't even thought about it. It was his birthday. So much had happened in the last few days, he hadn't even thought about his birthday. He wondered if he'd get new shoes, or some pants at suppertime. Birthdays were always the days he got new clothes. He didn't say anything, he just drank his milk and wiped off the white mustache with the back of his hand.

Irma poured herself a cup of coffee, and held the pot over the other mug. "Would you like a cup of coffee, Jim? I think a thir-teen-year-old boy is old enough to drink coffee." She gave him a broad smile. He was tall enough to look directly into her eyes. He hadn't noticed ever being that tall before.

"Yeah, sure, Mom," he said slowly. He wasn't too sure about cof-fee. "Is it as awful as it smells?" He really didn't want to drink the stuff. She and his father drank it all day long, but she'd never let him as much as taste it before. He figured maybe he really was an adult, and drinking coffee was what adults do. She poured a stream of the steaming brown liquid into the white cup. "You never put sugar in your coffee in the morning. Sugar after dinner, but never before." He stored the valuable adult information and picked up the steaming cup.

He put the brim under his nose and sniffed. It was awful. Irma's coffee was very strong and it had a bitter smell that stung the inside of his nose. He blew away the steam and slurped up a small mouthful. Mostly, it was hot. But the taste was not unpleasant, and it would be good if it had some sugar in it. He took another slurp, and looked over the mug to find his mother admiring him.

"I guess I couldn't tan your hide, after all, Jim. I think I'd like to call you Jim from now on. I think you're growin' up, son. You're nearly a man, now. I expect you'll be *working* like one before long." She was looking at her hand on the table, and her other hand held the coffee cup close to her face. Jimmy did the same. He supposed that coffee should never be too far from your face in case you want a drink.

He couldn't believe what she was saying. He was a kid! He wasn't an adult. At least, he didn't *feel* like an adult. He felt like a kid, and that was okay with him. Adults all had too much to worry about, and he wasn't quite ready to start worrying.

Irma continued, "When my momma was thirteen years old, she was engaged to be married to my daddy," she laughed. "I guess it's different with girls. When a girl is thirteen, sometimes she's gotta be all grown up."

Jimmy tried to imagine being engaged to be married. He didn't even know any girls. Unless you counted Madge Harrow. Or Margaret Price. Or, he thought, Hazel McPherson. Hazel McPherson was fourteen, and she looked like an adult. Last year she'd been a skinny kid, but all of a sudden, she was all grown up. She didn't act like a kid any more, and she didn't look like one either.

"I don't think I'm quite ready to get married, Ma." He didn't think that she was serious about the getting married part, but he wanted to check.

"No, but maybe you're ready to drink coffee, that's all. It's just that..." She was uncomfortable, she wasn't used to saying what was on her mind, except when she was angry. "Your time is coming, son. It's different when you're grown. I can't explain it, but it's different." She set down her coffee and played with her wedding ring.

"You're responsible for things. There's nobody to clean up after you. So you've got to look after things yourself." Jimmy couldn't believe this was his mother talking. "That's why we need to have neighbors, to look after each other. There's nobody else is going to make things work. People have got to stick together. You'll know all about it soon enough. I've seen you growin' up already. I've even caught you looking at young Hazel McPherson!"

Jimmy felt his face go red. He was stunned by his mother's words. He thought about Hazel McPherson and felt himself turn redder still.

"It's nothing to be ashamed of, Jim. As we grow up, our ideas about things change. We can't go through life all on our own, and the Good Lord means us to go through our life two by two. That's the way things are planned. You'll know all about it when the time is right." She gulped her coffee and walked to the counter, where her gigantic lunch basket was standing. Jimmy hoped she was finished talking about growing up. He'd heard some of this growing up stuff from Ralph Otis' big brother, and he didn't think he wanted to hear any more.

"Help me get this basket on to the buggy, will you Jim? Then you go on ahead to Mr. Wagner's place. Hal and I will be along shortly."

They lifted the heavy basket off the table and bumped it through the back door and up onto the waiting buggy. "I don't know where your father and brother have gotten to," she grumbled. She strode through the kitchen door and called up the stairs to her tardy husband and son, "Wil, I need your help down here! Hal! Let's get a move on!"

Walking over to Butts' place, Jimmy couldn't help thinking. He wasn't sure who he was anymore. Three days ago, he'd been

Jimmy Fox, but since then, he'd been called James, Jimmy, and Jim. He wasn't sure who he was supposed to be.

He was thinking about what his mother had said. Not just about Hazel McPherson, but about having nobody to look after him. He never really thought about who looked after his mom and dad. They were, well, adults and were there to look after, not to be looked after. He never really considered that one day he would be an adult; that he'd have to fret and worry. He didn't really feel any different being thirteen, either.

He rubbed his fingers, somehow thinking they might be thicker, stronger today. He thought about Hazel McPherson, and how she must feel to be so different all of a sudden. He wondered about who would look after him, and he started to worry a little.

13

Herring, Mr. Wagner?

Jimmy arrived at the Wagner barn to find the front doors swung back, the side doors open wide and all the windows propped open with long, thin poles.

Inside, a cool breeze gently blew through the stacks of lumber and supplies. Tall chairs on wheels were standing around the bat machine, and the long table in the workshop was covered with tins of paint and a wide variety of rags, pans, and brushes. Butts had rigged a criss-cross system of ropes and pulleys from the ceiling, with the bat rack hung near the end. A motor, exactly like the one on the elevator, sat between the bat machine and the painting room. Everything was ready.

"Ready to go to work James?" Butts called from the far end of the barn.

"Yes, sir. I'm ready," Jimmy called back. "My mom and Hal will be comin' by the lane. They oughtta be here any time now. What do you want me to do?" Jimmy expected that he'd be doing a real day's work today. He didn't expect to be playing any baseball, but then, with Butts Wagner, you never knew what to expect.

"I met your mother last night on the main road, and she told me to set the wheels in motion. I don't know how she did it, son, but she says she's got a crew comin' in here this morning to inaugurate the Wagner Baseball Equipment Company. You're a lucky boy, James. That's some mother you've got there."

His voice was getting closer. "She told me something else, too." He appeared around the end of a large wooden box, dressed from head to foot in a brand new black overall with red lettering on the chest. It said "Wagner Baseball Equipment Company." His black cap had a red button on the top, and a W on the front.

"She tells me that today is your thirteenth birthday. You know in some places, a boy who's thirteen years old is a man... Well, anyways, happy birthday, James Fox." He was holding out a piece of white paper.

"Thanks, Mr. Wagner. What is it?"

"It's just a memento of the day, James. Congratulations."

Jimmy opened up the carefully folded paper, and looked at the small rectangle of colored cardboard. It was a cigarette card. On it was a baseball player with "Pittsburgh" written across his chest. Underneath were the words "Wagner — Pittsburgh". Jimmy figured it must mean something to Butts, so he was glad to have it, but he thought it was a strange sort of birthday gift. He inspected the crisp card carefully. It looked a little like Butts, but it wasn't him.

Butts didn't give him the chance to say anything. "I know it ain't his best card," Butts explained, "but he sent it to me for my birthday. I want you to have it, James. May it give you many happy returns. One day you can give *me* a card with *your* brother's picture on it." Butts laughed, and slapped his leg. "Can you see it? Harold on a baseball card?"

Jimmy thought about it and grinned at Butts. "I don't think so, Butts." Jimmy was laughing at the idea of Hal on a baseball card, his smirky face grinning and his pudgy little hands gripping a Wagner Whacker.

"Well, this is *my* kid brother. He was just like Harold. He never stopped askin' questions." His face had a dreamy look, and his toothpick was in full spin. "I think I got to know so much just by having to keep up with Honus' questions.

"You know, he always had questions, and well, I was the older brother. I was supposed to know the answers. So I'd tell him he'd have to do something for me, and then I'd give him the answer. That way, I had time to find it out. And I didn't have anybody I could ask, you see. So I learned to read. We had a library in Pittsburgh, and I took to reading everything. I think I must have read every book in town before I was fifteen years old.

"That's when I joined up with pro baseball. At fifteen, I was grown, and I was expected to make a living. I knew how to answer nearly any question anybody could ask me, but the only thing I knew how to *do* was play baseball. It wasn't much, and most of the players spent what they earned, but we loved it.

"It was good baseball, no question. I was a long way from the big leagues, but over the years, I learned about the players in the game. Sure, I know how to play, and I was darned good, too, but what I learned on the way up was how to watch others play the game. By the time the Washington Senators found me, I was ready for them. I was a good hitter, but it was mostly 'cause I knew what to look for in pitchers. I'd been watching them. It's always the little things that'll give away a pitcher. It's the way his nose twitches, or the little grunt as the ball leaves his hand that tells you what he's throwing.

"I didn't have too much time for reading, so reading baseball games was what I did with my time on third base. I watched how the hitters gripped the bat, how they ground their feet into the dirt, and how they crouched.

"You see, Honus was a very good batter, even as a young boy, and he'd always ask me for my opinion of the height of his elbows, or his choke on the bat. I watched the other players mostly to be able to give tips to Honus. I don't mean to say I wasn't interested myself, but I guess it was having to explain something to somebody else that made me study things so carefully. Honus still asks me a hundred questions every time I see him. Here he is, the greatest baseball player who ever lived, and he needs to ask his big brother what he's doin' wrong against some two-bit left-handed pitcher from Wisconsin!

"You would be amazed at the scientific principles employed in baseball, James. Baseball players don't know it, but what they are doing can be explained, and *improved* on by studying the scientific principles behind it. I guess you don't want to talk about scientific principles on your birthday, though, do you James?"

Jimmy was sucking up every word. He really didn't understand everything Butts was saying, but he loved to hear him yammer along in his sing-song twang. "Sure, Butts," he lied, "It don't matter if it's my birthday."

Butts interrupted him. "There's just one more thing about scientific principles. That card you're holding. It's nearly one of a kind!" Butts wagged his head and chuckled. "Honus knows that tobacco and baseball are a bad combination. Tobacco makes your heart beat hard and fast, and in baseball, you've got to have a slow, steady heartbeat. Honus knows this (I told him, of course), though too many ballplayers use the stuff.

"So when this here tobacco company made up all these baseball cards to put in their tobacco packages, Honus made such a stink, that they had to unpack all the boxes and take out the cards. They were so mad that the owners of the club got involved. Anyway, Honus sent me that card as a memento of his brush with the National League Commissioner. I bet there ain't fifty like that in existence. Ol' Honie, he had 'em burn the whole lot!" Butts laid his arm around Jimmy's shoulders and walked him toward the door of the barn.

"So happy birthday, James." He extended his hand to the boy, and gripped it firmly, like one man to another.

Jimmy carefully folded the thick white paper around the baseball card, and slipped it into his shirt pocket. He understood how important the card was to Butts. If Hal had a baseball card, and there were no others like it, it would be very important to Jimmy. He patted his pocket to make sure the card was safe, and smiled at the thought of Hal on the front of a baseball card.

The two men, Butts Wagner and James Fox, headed out of the barn to greet Irma and the fidgety Hal. Jimmy had sunk so deep into his own thoughts that he hadn't heard the horse and buggy pull up.

Hal jumped off the wagon and started tugging at the picnic basket tied to the back. "Come on, Jimmy, help me get this thing off! I wanna see what's for lunch."

"You've just had your breakfast, Hal! I think you've lost your appetite and found a donkey's!" said Irma. She was standing with her hand on her hip, shaking her head. "You just leave that basket where it is. Jim, why don't you and your brother take care of the horse and buggy."

"G'mornin' Mrs. Fox," said Butts, tipping his baseball cap. "You really think we can do it, Irma?" He had one eye closed against the early morning sun.

"I think these ladies can handle just about anything you can imagine, Mr. Wagner. You just tell us what you want us to do and watch." She looked down the road to where a wagon was coming into sight. "That'll be Pip Van Droten. She makes the most wonderful sauerkraut..."

"So how many women did you find to work for a promise, Mrs. Fox?" Butts asked politely.

"Well, I just put the word out, Mr. Wagner. I can't say exactly who will come... I know we'll have Wil comin' by lunch time. And Pip, well that makes four of us..." She was smiling like she knew more than she was saying.

"Well," Ol' Man Wagner muttered, "I just wanted to know how many caps to get out."

"Have you got a box of twenty-four, Mr. Wagner?"

"Twenty-four! Twenty-four caps? Twenty-four women?" Butts stared hard into the distance. Jimmy followed his eyes to the road where they could see a small buggy with two heads bobbing in it. Behind it came a long wagonload of neighbors. The four of them stood watching as a parade of buggies and wagons came into sight. They could hear the voices of many women singing and laughing in the distance. Butts whistled between his teeth.

"Mrs. Fox, I think I'm gonna need a case of forty-eight!" He slapped his thigh and headed into the barn. "Harold, I could use some help here! Forty-eight caps!"

"Jim," said Irma as he unhitched the horse, "I want you to organize the horses. You'll have plenty of help, but you might want to take some of the animals across to our place." She gave Jimmy his morning marching orders and walked down the lane a little way to greet Mrs. Van Broten.

Butts and Hal came out of the barn, each carrying two small black cartons, as the parade of women, children and the odd husband, rolled into the Wagner yard.

"This is Elma Ferguson," Irma said, introducing Butts to a woman who'd just arrived at the barn door. Elma was as wide as she was tall, and she had a big, chubby smile. Butts handed her a cap and shook her hand.

"Welcome to the Wagner Baseball Equipment Company, Mrs. Ferguson," he said.

"The pleasure is mine, Mr. Wagner," she giggled. She pulled the brim of the cap down over her eyes and stepped aside for the woman behind her.

"Butts Wagner, Lucy McPherson," said Irma. He bowed, shook her hand and handed her a cap. Mrs. McPherson was dressed in her husband's overalls. She was nearly six feet tall, and had an uncontrollable head of red hair which would never fit under a baseball cap. She had it tied tight and knotted on the top, but even then she couldn't keep all the springy curls from spilling out here and there.

"Fine mornin' Mr. Wagner," she said cheerfully. "I guess it's a little late, but welcome to Fergus." She looked over at the house and nodded. "Mrs. Thompson, who lived here before you, was a friend of my mother's. I can't tell you how many afternoons I spent running through your barn, Mr. Wagner, I could tell you stories!" She laughed, pulling the cap over her red curls, and turned to the colorful figure bobbing up and down behind her.

Gladys Periwinkle wore a large yellow hat, a green and black polka dot dress and a red apron. She didn't look like she was dressed to work in a baseball equipment factory. She looked more like she was ready for a harvest dance. "Herring, Mr. Wagner?" she peeped. She had a voice exactly like a bird. Maybe a canary, or a Baltimore oriole.

"Pardon me, Ma'am?" Butts stammered. His pink lips were trembling behind his polite smile, ready to burst out laughing. He didn't know about Gladys Periwinkle's famous pickled herring.

"Herring?" she repeated, handing Butts a gray crock the size of a bread box. "Would you like a pickled herring, Mr. Wagner?" Her voice was so chirpy he couldn't help but laugh out loud.

"Thank you, Mrs. Periwinkle, why..." Butts sniffed the crock of pickled fish. It smelled like the locker room after a double header. "Not for breakfast, I think, but thank you." He bowed, accepting the contribution.

"Now, what was it you wanted us to do?" she trilled.

Irma Fox stepped in quickly, taking Mrs. Periwinkle and the pickled herrings along to the side of the barn where food tables were being set up. "Mr. Wagner will explain it all in good time, Gladys. Meanwhile, why don't you help Mrs. Costner organize the food?"

One by one, the women and the few husbands were introduced to Butts, who graciously welcomed each of the neighbors and handed each one a cap. For the first time since Jimmy had met him, Butts Wagner looked uncomfortable.

Butts led the small crowd into the barn and stood on a chair. He waved his arms calmly, and a hush fell over the room. "First of all, I'd like to thank you all for comin' out here." He looked around at all the new faces, and tried to put names on them in his mind.

"Believe it or not, this is the Wagner Baseball Equipment Company." Everyone laughed. "Oh, our beginnings may be humble, but it's a solid enterprise, and with work, this may grow to be a thriving industry."

"It sure don't look like Mr. Thompson's barn!" shouted Lucy McPherson, creating more laughter.

"I don't suppose there's a better place to begin than to show you exactly what we're doing here. James, can you come and give me a hand here?" Jimmy was sitting on a crate at the edge of the crowd, and he jumped off and skittered proudly over to the bat machine.

Butts took a plank and set it into the start position on the machine. Jimmy took a smaller piece of the dark wood and set it on the other end. "OK, son, let'er rip!" Butts nodded to Jimmy. He took hold of the bright red knob and pushed it halfway along its steel track.

BAARRAAP! ZIGGAAP! HUNK HUNK HUNK BAAR-RAP! The machine came to life. The thin arms sprang into action and pulled the lumber down to the rolling cutters.

People gasped as the machine whined high and loud, sending a shower of wood chips around the room. If they thought Butts was a kook before, they had no reason to doubt his genius now, as a perfectly shaped baseball bat was lifted from the rollers and fed into the large hole in the middle of the table.

When the bat was finished, and the spiral twirled up inside, the arms set the bat on the rack, and Butts pulled a lever. The rack rose from the ground and was pulleyed across the barn and set down next to the table where the paint and brushes were laid out. Butts explained the principles of the machine, and how the paint had to be put on in layers. By now, he was a lot more comfortable with the situation. He had a toothpick spinning and was waving his arms around, giving detailed scientific explanations for every step of the process.

He marched everyone outside to the baseball diamond, and when the *oohs* and *ahhs* and good gracious, this is a baseball field!'s were finished, he handed out bats and gave swinging lessons. He said that if someone was to make a finely crafted product, they had to "understand the principles."

Hal and Jimmy were huddled with Ralph Otis and Walter McPherson, watching their mothers swing bats out on the field. The Fox brothers had seen some strange things over the past few days, but this took the cake. For nearly half an hour they watched as two dozen grown women in black baseball caps swiped at imaginary fastballs in the morning light.

By lunchtime the Wagner Baseball Equipment Company was in full production. The barn shook with the buzz of the bat machine, wood chips flew, and voices rose in laughter over the din. A growing pile of completed bats was being sorted into racks, and wheeled out into the sun for paint drying. Butts, Irma and Mrs. McPherson were moving around the machine. He was explaining exactly how all the cranks worked, and what should show on the dials. He had a piece of paper with different formulas on it. The two women nodded as he spoke.

"And for a left-handed batter, they generally shift their upper bodies back, so we want to have most of the weight of the bat around the fourteen-inch mark. Look..." He explained and the women nodded.

Jimmy couldn't hear what they were saying, but he could see that now Mrs. McPherson was asking a question, and Butts was holding his hands out in front, as though gripping a bat, nodding and explaining something in precise detail. Then somebody rang a bell and Hal was off like a shot. It was lunchtime.

14

Trouble...

L unch had been set out in the shade of the barn on long tables
made of saw horses and raw lumber. There were crocks of
lemonade, several potato salads, beans of every possible
description, chicken, cold pork roast, pickled beets, onions, carrots, and turnip, and, of course, herring.

When the feast had dwindled to dog scraps and leftovers, the
neighbors sat in the shade laughing and making fun of each
other's mistakes on the job. Butts was beaming over the large
rack of completed bats and the rows of partly finished ones. He
had Mrs. McPherson by the arm, and was leading her to the finished rack. She nodded and took one of the bats off the rack and
handed it to Butts. Jimmy was watching from across the yard.

"Ladies," Butts spoke loudly, and everyone turned toward him.
"Ladies, this is an important day." He had the bat over his shoulder, and was turning from side to side so that everyone could hear
him. "Today marks the last leg of my life-long dream. And you are
making it happen. I've spent much of my life moving from place
to place, and I guess I never came to understand what the word
'neighbor' means. I guess I always thought it meant somebody
who lived down the road. Today, I understand. And I thank you."

Some of the women started to clap, but Butts held up his hand.

"One day, we'll all look back on this as an important day. But
I think nobody will remember today better than the man who

made all this happen. I say 'man', because today, he becomes one. I'm talkin' about James Fox, who is thirteen years old today." Jimmy was shocked. Everybody was looking at him and smiling, and he didn't know what he was supposed to do.

"James, come on over here." Jimmy walked slowly across the grass into the bright sun where the old man was standing. "James, I want you to have this. This is the first bat manufactured by the Wagner Baseball Equipment Company. I have it on the best authority of Mrs. McPherson that this was the first bat to be lacquered and dried. May it bring you good luck always!" Jimmy took the hat and everyone laughed, cheered and clapped their hands.

The women drifted back into the barn, and slowly the sounds of grinding and sawing drowned out the singing and laughter. Jimmy sat at the home plate bench and carved his initials into the butt end of the bat. He had nearly finished the "F" when he glanced up at the road. At first all he saw was the glint of bright sun on glass, but soon he could see the familiar red car racing ahead of a trail of brown dust on the road. It was the Yankee thugs!

Jimmy jumped to his feet and tore off toward the barn, still gripping his bat. His head jerked from side to side in a frantic search for Butts' black cap and gray hair. He saw his mother in the paint shop and called out to her. "Where's Butts? I've got to find him!" He didn't want to tell anybody what he'd seen until he'd spoken to Butts. She pointed up with her thumb. He looked up and saw the elevator at the loft. That meant Butts had to be up there too. He dropped the bat at her feet, and ran across to the far side of the barn.

He gulped and grabbed the bottom rung of the ladder. Hand over hand, he scooted up the long ladder that never seemed to end. Finally, he reached the top and swung the hatch open. Butts was asleep.

Twenty women were grinding out Wagner Whackers, more were cleaning up the lunch, three thugs were rolling up the road to the farm, and Butts Wagner was sleeping. Jimmy ran over and shook him.

"Butts! For the love of Mike would you wake up! We've got *trouble*!" Butts' eyes popped open and he snorted loudly.

"What! What's goin' on, boy? I was having the best dream I've had in years. How'd you get up here? Oh," he said, looking at the open hatch door, "you came up the hard way. What seems to be the problem, James?"

"The problem," Jimmy panted, "is three guys from the loan company. I seen them comin' up the road! What are we gonna do?"

"Do?" Butts tried to look like he wasn't the least bit worried, but Jimmy knew better this time. "We're gonna talk to 'em." He went quiet for a long minute. "No, I don't think we'll talk to 'em. James, you get over to the window yonder and watch. You'll be the eyes." Jimmy looked where Butts was pointing. There was a huge window all right, but it might as well have been a hundred miles away. It was on the far side of the barn.

"Sure, Butts, but how do I get over there?"

"Over there? Oh, yeah. You've got to take the rope, James." He pointed to a fat rope which was hooked to the rail. It was tied high in the peak of the barn. Jimmy would have to stand on the rail, grab the rope, swing over the yawning gap, and land on the smaller platform on the far side.

"Y'ain't scared, are you James? I've done it myself a hundred times. I wouldn't ask you to do anything I wouldn't do myself." Jimmy's eyes gaped at the worried man. He gulped, turned to examine the space between where he was and where Butts wanted him to go. Butts' eyes burned through the back of his head, and his voice came like a ripple of dangerous water. "You've got to do it, James. I'm goin' down to put the ground forces into action. You're my eyes, boy. Now git."

Jimmy held onto the rope and climbed up onto the narrow rail. He looked down and saw his mother looking up at him. She was shouting something, but there was so much noise from the machine that he couldn't hear her. He knew what she was saying though, she was ordering him not to jump.

He gritted his teeth, gripped the rope, and shoved off, his feet gripping the fat knot in the rope. The other platform seemed a lot further away when he was spinning in midair than when he stood in the relative safety of Butts' living room. The warm air whooshed against his terrified face and his numb fingers. As the far platform closed in, he forced one foot out to get a toe-hold on the rough wooden plank. First one foot, then the other, clung to the platform. He'd made it! He fastened the rope to the post, and raced to the windows. By now Butts had arrived on the floor, and the machine had come to a stop.

Jimmy wiped away the dirt and grime from one of the lower panes. The long red car was rolling up the driveway, and Jimmy turned to call out to Butts. As he turned, his shirt caught on a nail. Two buttons popped off and the carefully folded birthday gift slipped from his torn pocket and fell onto a strut below the window frame. Too excited to notice the torn shirt or lost baseball card, Jimmy crept to the edge of the platform and called to the silent crowd down below. "They're here!"

Then he returned to the window to watch Butts strut across to meet the red car. The rear door swung open and Jingo The Shooter jumped out before the car came to a full stop. He pointed a finger at Butts and grinned nastily. Butts stood with his hands on his hips and nodded. The other two men got out and stretched their legs. The one called Louie rubbed his fist into his palm, and the other one, the big driver with the mustache, wiped his forehead with a limp white handkerchief. Butts was wagging and pointing, but clearly standing his ground. Suddenly, two of the men grabbed Butts from either side, and Louie punched him in the stomach.

As Butts tore himself free, Jimmy saw a stream of black caps pour out of the barn in the direction of the car. He scuttled to the edge of the platform, grabbed the rope and swung cleanly to the far side of the barn, tumbling over the rail and onto the floor of the loft. He ran to the open hatch and swung down onto the ladder. Pulling the door closed behind him, he hurried down to the ground.

Outside it was chaos. Mrs. Periwinkle had handed out Wagner Whackers from the drying rack, and bat-toting farmwives were all over, chasing two of the men around the property. The men had a jump on them though, and were crossing into the Fox's back acres. Butts was leading the chase in his black and red overalls. Everybody, including Hal and Ralph Otis, was out in the field. Jimmy ran to the wood pile, grabbed a stout piece of bat lumber and joined the chase.

"Hey kid!" Jimmy spun around. "Don't move, kid, I've got a gun." The thug was crouched out of sight behind the machine.

"I ain't movin'. What d'ya want me to do?"

"So you can speak English, huh? I knew I should'a shown you the barrel of my gun, and not the color of my money. Drop the wood. Careful like." Jimmy dropped it by his feet. "Come over here where I can see you better. You're just gonna wait here with me while I figure the best way to get out of here."

Jimmy saw the top of a hat rise up from behind the machine. It was Louie, the gangster boss. Sweat was running down his fat face, soaking his scruffy mustache and his chins. "Get over here. And don't say a word." He waved his gun at Jimmy, signalling him to come around the machine. Jimmy obeyed, squatting down at the corner near the motor. He didn't want to get any closer to Louie than he had to.

"Just stay there, kid. And shut up while I figure this out." He set the gun up on the bat rack and wiped the sweat from his eyes. He nodded at the machine. "What is this thing, anyway, kid? This Wagner is some kind of kook, ain't he?" Louie twisted his sweaty lips into a sneer. "Well, my boss, he ain't a kook. He's a business man. And he wants his money. He don't want it all rolled up in some cockamamie piece of junk in Canada." Louie rubbed his dripping face and neck with a huge pocket handkerchief. "So what is this thing, anyway?" he repeated.

Jimmy had to think fast. "Why, this is a money makin' machine, mister. This machine can make a hundred dollars in less than five minutes. I could make, oh, maybe a thousand dollars right now, before anybody got back from chasing your friends across the field."

"A money makin' machine? Come on, kid, he ain't that kooky. Wagner told you that?"

"It's true. I've seen it workin'. Why d'ya think all these people come around to help him? Yes sir, we're all gonna be rich around here. They just took the first load off to the bank at lunchtime." Jimmy rubbed the machine with his sleeve. "Ya wanna see it work?"

"It can't make dollar bills outta lumber. Can't be done."

"I could show ya, mister. I know how to run it."

"Okay, kid, let's see you make me a thousand dollars!" The big man laughed and spat onto the hard dirt floor.

Jimmy pulled the red knob. BAARRAAP! ZIGGAAP! HUNK HUNK HUNK BAARRAP! The machine burped to life. He pulled another switch, bringing the smaller motor into action. The bat rack rose from the ground, taking the gun with it, and when it was well out of the man's reach, Jimmy pulled the lever to the bat rack and killed the motor.

"Why you lousy..." Louie was jumping for his gun, and Jimmy ducked down behind the table. The bat machine was in high gear, arms swinging and wood chips flying. He couldn't hear the fat thug over the noise, but he had to find out where Louie was. And he had to be fast.

He spotted something on the ground, near the end of the machine. It was the bat with his initials carved in the end. He had dropped it when his mother pointed him up to the loft to find Butts. He scooted along the dirt floor and grabbed it. Through the side door Jimmy could see Butts and all the women leading the two stumbling crooks across the field.

Out of the corner of his eye, he saw Louie's feet shuffling around at the other end of the machine. He was pushing and pulling levers, trying to get the bat rack down, but so far, all he was doing was increasing the speed of the clattering claw-arms.

"Jimmy!" He heard his brother's voice and jumped to his feet. "Hal, get out of here!" Louie laughed from the far end of the rolling table. Hal was headed straight into Louie's fat arms. "Hal! No! Get out of here! Fast!" he called.

As he yelled, he could see the steel arm swinging straight at his forehead. He dove out of its path. Hal spun around and raced out of the barn, and as Jimmy hit the ground he saw Butts running in from the baseball field.

"The gun!" Jimmy roared. "It's in the bat rack."

"I don't need a gun where the likes of this fellow are concerned." Butts spoke calmly, staring at the fat, sweaty, thug. He pulled the lever, bringing the machine to a grumbling halt. "Come on, James, get on up and come over here." Jimmy jumped to his feet and dusted himself off.

"And you, Sir," he said to Louie, "You half-witted messenger-boy, you can get on outta here and join your buddies in the car. You can tell your Mr. Hogg that I'll get him his money. Every nickel of it. No Wagner has ever welshed on a deal before, and I ain't about to begin a new family tradition. He'll get his money, but he's just gonna have to wait for it. Now get on yer way and don't come back without an invite."

Butts stepped forward and the man took off like a shot. Jimmy heard the car door slam and the engine roar out of the yard. For a minute, everything was dead quiet. Then somewhere, somebody burst out laughing. It wasn't funny, but just the same nobody could keep from laughing with relief.

When the afternoon shift got back to work, everybody seemed to be more serious about what they were doing. It seemed to Jimmy that all these people really cared about Butts and about the job that needed to be done. For the next few days, this wasn't to be the Old Thompson Place, and these neighbors weren't farm women, this was the Wagner Baseball Equipment Company.

15

Honus

I t was late when Jimmy heard the truck rumble up the drive. He was supposed to be sleeping, but he was too excited to close his eyes. He had lain in the dark since nine o'clock, wondering what tomorrow would have in store for him. Nothing was the same anymore. He used to dread Sundays, dressing up in his best clothes and going to church. Now he couldn't wait for Sunday. On Sunday, in just a few hours, he would be in Watertown, New York, watching the Pittsburgh Pirates and the Watertown Mohawks play baseball.

Mr. Van Dorp had given Butts his truck for the trip. Butts figured that it would take twelve hours to get to Watertown, and that they would have to cross the river during the daylight, so they were to leave at eleven o'clock tonight. Butts planned to reach Kingston by morning, and make the crossing to Wolfe Island on the first boat. The drive across Wolfe Island to the American ferry would be short, and that ferry would bring them nearly all the way to Watertown. Jimmy listened for Butts to come in the back door, and he crept over to wake his brother.

"Hal, get up! He's here!"

"I wasn't sleepin', I was just waitin' for Butts to get here." Hal rubbed his eyes and slid into his pants.

"You were snoring, Hal." Jimmy knew he wouldn't win an argument with Hal about whether or not he was sleeping, or snor-

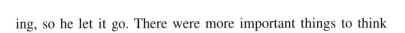

ing, so he let it go. There were more important things to think about. "Okay, I know, you snore when you're awake."

"Yeah." Hal was going to let it drop too. "I feel like breakfast. D'ya think mom'll give us something to eat in the truck?" In fact, she had packed a picnic hamper for their journey. As usual, there was enough food to keep the three of them stuffed for a month of Sundays.

"Don't worry about it, Hal. Eating'll be about the last thing we have to think about. I know Mrs. Periwinkle is sending along a jar of pickled herring. Want me to bring it up in the cab with us?"

"Yuk. Pickled herring." Hal scrunched up his face and stuck out his tongue.

"What is pickled herring, anyway?" Hal was bending out the window, looking down into the truck parked below. The bright moon lit up the tops of the crates and boxes, all tied down with chains to the bed of the truck. Hal had been in Mr. Van Dorp's truck before, but this was going to be different.

"It's a fish," Jimmy said, watching Hal and buttoning his shirt. "It smells very bad. That's why Mrs. Periwinkle kills them and puts them in jars. Because they smell bad." Jimmy knew what Hal's next question would be. "And I don't know why anyone eats them. They're smelly fish. I don't know why anybody would eat a smelly fish." Hal was silent, apparently satisfied with the explanation.

"Anyway," Jimmy said, "we should go down. Butts is probably waiting for us. It's probably eleven o'clock."

Jimmy opened the door and Hal bolted through it, turning to wait at the top of the stairs. As they came down, they could hear the adults murmuring quietly in the kitchen. When Butts talked quietly, it sounded like a giant bumble bee buzzing. He filled the whole room with sound, but his voice was soft, like velvet.

The warm smell of fresh coffee and muffins filled the kitchen. A large platter stood on the table. When the two boys entered, Irma put muffins on plates for them, and they sat down quietly as Butts continued talking.

"I've got the two sets ready, and packed up. You know, Irma, I think we've got two near-perfect sets of bats. I've tested each and every one of 'em, and they all respond exactly as they should.

This is going to be some ball game. Just you wait!

"Hiya, boys. You're ready to go?" Butts smiled at Jimmy and Hal, and crunched up his face into a sort of pained grin. "The best time to start a journey is on time and that, my boys, is right now. Any last minute trips out back should start about now." Hal slunk out of the kitchen, but Jimmy just kissed his mother, grabbed a muffin, and headed for the truck.

Very soon they were miles from home, bumping through the black countryside. Jimmy leaned against the cool steel door, keeping himself alert by watching the roadside brush disappear into darkness. Butts sat erect with both hands on the wheel, toothpick flipping between his lips, and Hal slumped in between the two of them, snoring quietly.

When he awoke, Jimmy was staring across the wide, blue Lake Ontario morning. Butts was standing at the side of the road with his hands on hips, looking out over the water. Jimmy opened the truck door and slid down onto the dirt track.

"Across there, James, my boy, that's my home. The United States of America. Best darned country in the world. No offense, of course. It's my home, and well, a man should always believe in his country. Even if he don't live there."

Jimmy realized he must have slept through the first ferry crossing onto the island, and they were standing on the far side of Wolfe Island, looking across at the American shore.

Butts had a toothpick going. "You want something to eat? Your brother and I have had our breakfast. He's just down the hill seein' a man about a dog."

"He's doin' what?" Jimmy hoped that Hal hadn't talked Butts into letting him have another dog. "What dog?"

Butts clicked his tongue and shook his head at Jimmy. "Call a'nature, James." Jimmy still didn't get it. "Had to pee, for Pete's sake!"

"Oh, yeah," Jimmy said. He helped himself from the food hamper, and Butts chattered on about the next leg of the journey. "So we cross over down the road a piece, and we'll end up," he pointed far across the lake and wiggled his finger, "just about there.

From the far side, it shouldn't be more than two hours' drive to Watertown, an' by the time we get unloaded, we'll have just about enough time to meet all the boys before the game."

They packed up quickly and headed the truck down the hill and along the water's edge to the ferry landing. They arrived at the dock in plenty of time for the crossing, and the boys played at being pirates, attacking sleek Yankee schooners on the high seas.

The land on the American side of the water was a series of rolling hills. They sang rounds and slapped their knees in time to Butts' whistling. When Watertown finally appeared from the top of a very high hill, the cab of the truck went silent. Butts stopped whistling, Hal sat with his hands folded, and Jimmy gripped the baseball Butts had brought along for luck. In a couple of hours, he thought to himself, the greatest baseball team ever was going to play a game using the finest collection of baseball bats ever assembled. They could smell baseball in the air.

The baseball field was in the center of Watertown. The opening pitch was set for one o'clock, and already, at eleven in the morning, there were cars, trucks, horses, buggies, and people everywhere. Jimmy couldn't remember seeing so many people in his life. Hal didn't like it.

"There's an *awful* lot of people here, Mr. Wagner." He stared, slack-jawed, out into the parade of farmers, ladies, well-dressed gentlemen and kids.

"Wouldn't be much of an *exhibition* if there weren't a lot of *people*, now would it, Harold?" Butts nosed the truck up behind the grandstand, and through to where a man was standing at the end of a row of barrels. The barrels were a sort of a fence, and the man stood with his hands around a rifle, letting people know that this was out of bounds. Butts pulled the truck up to the barrels, and stuck his head out the window.

"G'mornin'. We're expected, son." The man with the gun tipped his hat back off his forehead and strolled over to the side of the truck.

"Whatcha got here, mister? If you're wantin' to sell some goods, they're settin' up over to the side, off 9th Avenue."

"This is *baseball* business, friend. We're the Wagner Baseball Equipment Company. Albertus Wagner, at'chyer service." Butts all of a sudden sounded more like an American than ever.

"Wagner? *Butts Wagner?* Well, I'll be!" The man smiled a big, toothy smile and wagged his head. "I'm *real* glad to meet'chu-all, Mr. Butts Wagner. Why don't you just *drive* on through. I think your brother's gonna be *real* glad to see you Mr. Wagner." He scratched the side of his face and repeated himself. "Mr. Butts Wagner." He tucked the rifle under his arm and took off his hat. Bending at the waist he swept his hat through the opening in the barrels, and Butts drove on in.

Jimmy just stared at Hal, who was as wide-eyed as he was. They grinned at each other, delighted at being in such highly prized company. Butts had said that people in America would know who he was, but Jimmy didn't expect they'd treat him like the President! Butts bumped over the fresh-cut grass to the back of the stadium where large tents and roped-off areas were set up for the teams, and for the town big shots. There were several large tents with red, white and blue streamers tied up on the sides.

There were people everywhere. There was a very fat man with a black and white suit that didn't cover his hairy stomach. There was a tiny man in a tiny baseball uniform with towels over his shoulder who seemed to be everywhere at once. Two women in very large hats stood in the sunshine drinking lemonade and watching the parade of people passing by them. There were several men with dollar bills sticking out from between their fingers. They were calling out numbers and taking money and giving out small slips of paper to tall men and fat men, men with mustaches, short men with beards, men with tall hats, flat hats and men in their Sunday dress. The two boys from Fergus drank up the Annual Watertown Baseball Exhibition Game with wide eyes and silent dreams.

The tiny man with the towels poked his head under the rope and came out to meet the truck. "Butts Wagner?" he grinned. The little man was only about the same size as Hal. His voice was as strange as his appearance. Jimmy thought he sounded like the squeak of a dry hinge on a barn door.

"Yessir. The Wagner Baseball Equipment Company," Butts replied, turning the motor off in the truck.

"You're expected, Mr. Wagner," he creaked, "just follow me." The little man ducked back under the rope and headed off through the crowd. Butts, Jimmy and Hal took off at a run to catch up with him. They passed the two ladies with big hats and Butts tipped his cap and smiled as he ran past them. The men with money in their fingers called out numbers to Butts, but he ignored them. Jimmy could see the little towel man darting through the crowd. When they finally caught up with him, he was standing outside a long, wide tent, and as they puffed up to the doorway, he pulled the flap open for them and bowed at the waist.

When the three of them stepped into the gloomy tent from the bright sunshine, they couldn't see a thing. Their eyes took some time to adjust to the change. A big, booming voice called out, laughing, "Well, if it ain't Butts Wagner himself! Ha ha!"

Butts knew that laugh. "If that ain't Donie Bush, I'm Jack the Bear!" Butts hollered. The man stepped forward and they shook hands and slapped each other on the shoulder. Jimmy stood next to Butts, and Hal stood right behind him on the other side.

"These are my men, James and Harold Fox." Butts pushed Hal ahead of him, keeping his hand over the back of Hal's head. Jimmy stepped forward and took the man's outstretched hand. He liked being called one of the men.

"James, this is Donie Bush, manager of the best baseball club ever assembled. Harold, say hello to Donie. He's as good a man, and as fine a baseball player as ever a man has been." Hal shook Donie's hand and looked at his boots.

"Hal wears Whitey Lumbart's old jersey," Butts explained.

"Whitey Lumbart. Good man." Donie bent down and looked at Hal. "You a second baseman, Harry? You could do worse than wear Ol' Whitey Lumbart's jersey."

Just then, Donie turned his head as a big man strode up to the front of the tent. "Well, boys, here's our man now!"

"Well, if it ain't my own brother Albert! Hiya, Buttsie! My, my, my, Butts, but don't you look a sight with your gray head! What would mama say about that?" He was laughing and gave his brother a big handshake, and pulled him in for a back-slapping hug.

"Honie boy, you'll git yours. Just you wait 'til you're as old and wise as I am." The two of them stood looking at each other and smiling for a long time. Then Butts spoke. "Honus, I'd like you to meet my men. This is James and Harold Fox. James, Harold, this is my little brother, the great Honus Wagner. Honie's on the management side of the organization these days, but he'll be in the lineup today, wontchya baby brother?" Butts' 'baby brother' nodded and smiled, grinding one enormous fist into the palm of the other. "I wouldn't miss it for the world, Albert. I'll be playin' short stop, just like the old days."

The greatest baseball player of all time stood before them with his hands on his hips. He wore a clean, starched baseball shirt with the word Pittsburgh sewn across the front. He looked exactly like the man on the card Butts had given to Jimmy.

Two weeks ago, Jimmy Fox had never heard the name Honus Wagner. He had never been a big baseball fan. He didn't know about baseball royalty. Now, standing not three feet away was a man who was as important in America as the Queen was in Canada. He wasn't sure what he was supposed to do. Was he supposed to bow? Take his cap off? Or just shake his hand? He didn't need to worry about it. Hal had grabbed Honus' gigantic hand and was pumping away.

"Glad to meet you, Honus," Hal chirped. The men all broke up laughing, and Honus squatted down to Hal's level and shook his hand and rubbed his head.

"Glad to meet you, too, Harold Fox."

Donie Bush chuckled at Hal and Honus. "Harold wears Whitey Lumbart's old jersey," he said. He turned to Hal. "Now, Honus could tell you a tale about Whitey Lumbart, Harry! Don't you tell a story about Whitey Lumbart?"

Butts turned to Honus, who was shaking Jimmy's hand. "Ya, Honie, tell us about your first day at short stop. Whitey was at second, wasn't he?" Honus was grinning and shaking his head. "Naw," he laughed, "Whitey was at the plate.

"Whitey Lumbart. That was when...who was it, now?" He scratched his head for a minute. "It was Bob Emsley behind the pitch. Bob Emsley. As wise and crafty an umpire as you'll ever see. Like my brother says," Honus stood up tall and laid his enormous hand on his big brother's shoulder. "It was my first day at short stop. Sort of a tryout for the regular spot.

"We were ahead, it was late in the game, bottom of the eighth, it would'a been. Whitey Lumbart hits a deep bouncer between me and third. I can get to the ball, no problem. I head for the ball, and keep my eye on the runner at second. The runner looks for third, he's leaning, but he doesn't break; there's two out, so he ain't gonna break if he ain't sure... Well, meantime a dog has run in from somewhere in left field and she's got to the ball before I do. She's got the ball, and I got my eye on the runner. When he sees that the dog's got the ball, he breaks for third. I go for the ball, but the dog don't want to give it up, thinks I want to play. Well, I do, but not the way the dog had it figured. So I grabs the ball, dog and all, up in my arms, and I fling myself, dog first, at the oncoming runner, and I tag him, Fido an' all. The ump, Emsley, bless his heart, calls him out!

"He's out all right. Oh, they yelled, and argued all summer about it, but Emsley was right, the runner was out. The dog was in my hand, and the ball was in Fido's snout." Honus had the same pale blue eyes as Butts, and they sort of sunk back when he told the story, just like Butts' did. Honus laughed, and finished his story.

"So that was my first day at short stop! Playin' short stop has never been sweeter than that first sunny afternoon."

All the men laughed, but Jimmy and Hal didn't know whether the story was true, or just a good fib.

Donie Bush cleared his throat and spoke to Butts. "I don't like to break up the family reunion here, but we've got some business to discuss haven't we, Albert?" Donie called over the small towel man. He whispered something to the little man who scurried out of the room as quickly as his little legs would carry him.

Butts turned to Donie Bush and told him what he had in mind. "I'd like to sit with your equipment man, if you don't mind, Donie.

My boys, James and Harold, will work with the Watertown equipment man. They can explain how the system works."

The little towel man returned with a tall older man and a short, chubby younger one. They joined the small circle and were introduced as the manager of the Watertown team, and the umpire.

Butts explained what he had in mind. "I've brought two sets of Wagner Whackers with me. There's absolutely no difference between one and the other — that's a fact, a scientific fact. But just the same, I think it would be in order to allow the home team first choice, don't you think, Ump?"

The chubby young man nodded and looked around the small circle of faces. "Seems right to me, Mr. Wagner. 'Zat seem right to all?" Everyone nodded. Jimmy hadn't thought of who would get first pick. He was impressed that Butts had it all figured out, and that everybody agreed that it was fair.

It was a Sunday afternoon baseball exhibition, not a World Series Final, and the men who were gathered in the dark tent behind the right field stands didn't figure that the bats they were to use for the game were very important. As it turned out, however, they were wrong. The bats mattered. This was The Watertown Game.

16

The Watertown Game

Jimmy spent the next hour showing the Watertown bat boy how the system worked. He didn't know that much, but he knew which bats were for the long ball, and that's what the Watertown men wanted to know. Butts stood talking to the two managers and the players who came over to chat with him. From time to time, he'd lift a bat and shake it in his fists, or wave it over his head, or point off in the distance.

All around the field, people were packing up their lunches and finding places to watch the game. Hal was playing catch with one of the players' kids, and the umpire came out to move them off the diamond and call out the managers for the ground rules.

The Watertown team had a hard-throwing left-hander as the starting pitcher. The Pirates were using a right-hander. When the teams were announced and the bows all taken, the crowd fell silent, and Watertown's herky-jerky left-hander wound up and let go a fastball, high and outside. When the bat connected, the ball went out over the crowd and into the fairground. The crowd sent up a cheer for the visitors. The next pitch was smacked into the crowd deep in left field, and the score was 2-0 Pirates. The next hitter drove a long liner straight at the center fielder, who caught the ball for the first out. The fourth batter struck out, and the fifth sat down behind him.

The Pirates took the field, and got the first two outs swinging.

The third batter on the Watertown team was Yank Milson, a pro who was 'between professional assignments'. That, Jimmy was told, was baseball lingo for 'all washed up'. He looked at the first pitch, took the second as a strike, and took the third pitch all the way out. They don't know how far Yank Milson hit the ball. Nobody ever found it. Some people actually believe that the ball disintegrated. Jimmy sure didn't see where it landed. He had never seen anything go as far as the ball Yank Milson hit into downtown Watertown. It seemed to go out to where the road must have been, but he never saw it drop.

The crowd went wild. People were running onto the field shaking Yank Milson's hand and yelling, until somebody fired a shot, and the playing field emptied out. The next batter hit between second and third base, behind Honus, where nobody could get to it. He stopped at second base. The next batter was walked. The left-handed pitcher, Lionel McQuaid, came out to hit, and the crowd started calling his name.

"Lionel! Lionel! Lionel!" they hollered. The pitch was outside, but he reached across for it and sent it sailing above the right field crowd: 4-2, Watertown. The catcher hit a single, and was batted home by the eighth place hitter. He hit a rope to short stop, and Honus tossed the ball in and shook his head all the way to the dugout.

He looked over at Butts and shook his head again. He yelled something, but Jimmy couldn't hear what he said.

Jimmy followed Honus over to the Pirates' dugout to watch the great man choose his bat. Honus took a long time about it. Butts pointed at this one and that, and they settled on a bat with almost no spring. He chose what Butts called a line drive bat, and strutted out to the plate. "This'd better be a good bat, Buttsie."

Butts cupped his hands over his mouth and yelled out, "Do it the hard way baby brother!" and the whole team laughed.

Honus took the first pitch for a strike. The next pitch was inside, and he let it go by.

"Hey, Honus," Butts yelled "You've got to swing the dagnab'd thing. Else it won't work!"

The third pitch was a high strike. A home run ball. Honus just yelled over his shoulder, "Yeah, yeah, yeah." The next pitch was in the dirt.

The lefty gave nothing away, but threw a hard, sinking fastball. Honus waited on it. He could have left it for ball three, but he was doing it the hard way. He wound up and caught it at about knee level. The ball swept past the pitcher near enough to catch, but far too fast to see, and continued out over left center field where the outfielders were converging. The ball left the park at about the same height and speed as when it left Honus Wagner's bat.

They say it's a miracle that nobody was killed by the ball. It knocked the tripod out from under a camera, but nobody was hurt, and the photographer may have captured a rare moment in baseball history.

The Pirates scored six runs in the second inning. Watertown responded with eleven. Honus went six for six with two home runs. He wasn't the star of the game, however. Yank Milson, the home-town ringer, went six for six and hit five home runs.

The Watertown Game was decided in the tenth inning. The score was tied at 57 to 57, and nobody had scored since the eighth inning. The word spread like wildfire about Butts and the Wagner Whacker. The crowd kept calling for Butts to come out. Watertown took to the field for the bottom of the tenth inning and the crowd chanted "Wagner, Wagner, Wagner!"

Finally, after being pushed and shoved out of the dugout, Butts took a low bow, to the cheers and whistles of the thousands of men and women. He went back into the dugout, and the whistles and calls got louder. Nobody came out of the Pirates dugout, and the umpire walked over to see what was the matter.

When he came out, he was followed by Butts Wagner, his gray hair sticking out of his new Pittsburgh Pirates cap. Jimmy and Hal looked at each other. They couldn't believe that this was happening. Butts was going to bat!

He smiled out at the crowd, took another bow, and then bent low to the ground with his bat. He grabbed up a big handful of dirt and rubbed it into his hands. Then he pulled the cap down low over his eyes, and pointed the bat at the pitcher, as if to say "let'er rip".

The crowd was silent. Hal burped. The pitcher wound up and delivered a sizzling fastball. The ball seemed to travel in slow motion, floating into the strike zone like a lazy butterfly. The crowd held its breath as Butts lifted the bat from his shoulder and extended his long arms, smoothly bringing the bat around his body.

The catcher looked in his glove for the ball. He didn't see it hit the bat. He heard the smack of contact, but he couldn't believe that Butts had hit it. The old man hadn't swung hard enough.

Butts didn't swing the bat hard. He lifted his front foot, just slightly, and drove the ball right over first base. The umpire was yelling "Fair ball!" as he watched it zoom up the base path. It wasn't inside the first base line, it was *on* the first base line. The ball was hit so exactly they could have used that hit to draw out the field. Butts' home run sailed over the bag, high into right field, and hooked well into fair territory, far back into the crowd. A fat man in the picnic grounds bobbed up and down with the ball raised up over his head. The crowd cheered, whistled and stomped. The game was over.

There had never been another game like the Watertown Annual Baseball Exhibition Game of 1928. All the exhibition games before this one, and all games since, have been forgotten. Only this game is remembered, and there would never be another one like it. The records from The Watertown Game were never kept officially. Some say the story got exaggerated over time and the many retellings. Nobody really knows. What they say about The Watertown Game is that it was the most incredible day in the history of batting.

The players and fans swept up Butts, Jimmy and Hal and carried them, shouting and singing, to the town hall a few blocks away. The mayor stepped forward to make a speech when Donie Bush rushed in front of him and waved the crowd to silence. He had a speech of his own. Donie looked around him and nodded to the boys.

"Never," he began, "Never, in the history of our Grand Old Game has there been such a day for baseball. I have played baseball from one end of this country to the other. I've played with the greats in Detroit, in Cincinnati, in New York, and, of course, in Pittsburgh. But I have never seen baseball played as we have seen it played today.

"Ladies and gentlemen, this day will revolutionize baseball. From one of America's great baseball families has come the most impressive innovation the game has ever known. I lift my hat," and he took his cap off, and held it over his chest, "I lift my hat to Albertus J. Wagner, and his Baseball Equipment Company."

The crowd cheered and whistled. Jimmy clapped and stomped his feet as Butts took center stage. He waved his arms until people were quiet. "Thank you, ladies and gentlemen," Butts smiled. "I guess I'm not one for makin' public speeches, but I want to thank you for makin' my dream come true.

"I dreamed of today, and I went about trying to make it happen. I always knew it would, but I didn't know exactly when, or how. And it was supposed to happen like this." He wiped away a trickle from his cheek. "My men, the Fox brothers, and I are very proud to have been part of this great day.

"I want to thank you for your confidence and your hospitality..." Butts looked suddenly confused, like he had forgotten something important. He continued his rambling speech. "I don't know what happens next, but I suppose that's the way it is with dreams, and with real life. Ya don't know what happens next..."

The mayor could see that Butts was settling in for a long, dreamy chat with several hundred people, and he knew just what to do. He jumped forward, shouting "Three cheers for Butts Wagner!" The crowd was happy to join in, and the mayor gave up any thought of making a speech of his own.

The whole truth about The Watertown Game will probably never be known. Those who were there, and their grandchildren, say that the people of northern New York celebrated for six days, and only gave it up because the seventh day was Sunday.

Donie Bush walked the men from the Wagner Baseball Equipment Company to their truck, where the two cases of bats had already been loaded up. He handed Butts an envelope and a smile. In the distance, they could still hear the mayor and the big shots from both teams toasting one another. They would keep it up for many more hours, but Butts, Jimmy and Hal had to catch the last ferry across to the other side. Butts had had a good long walk with his brother, Honus, and Hal had had his fill of food from the Ladies Auxiliary tent. Jimmy had met most of the players on both teams, and had a new respect for baseball, and for the men and boys who played it.

As the truck pulled onto the open road, Butts looked over at the boys and stuck a toothpick into his twitching mouth. "Thank you James. Thank you Harold. I could never have done this without you boys and your family. Donie Bush and the Pirates have ordered enough bats to put us into full production. By this time next year, every team in the Major Leagues will carry a complete set of Wagner Whackers. I told you boys that we were gonna revolutionize baseball, and today, we set the baseball world spinnin'. This has been my finest hour."

17

Journey's End

They were quiet most of the way back to Fergus. Something was wrong with Butts. He didn't whistle, he didn't chew toothpicks, and he didn't tell stories. It was seven-thirty in the morning when the truck rumbled up the lane to the Fox's house. Irma was hanging up laundry, and Wil could just be seen out in the field. Jimmy didn't remember the farm ever looking so green and beautiful.

The boys slipped out of the truck as their mother came up and began telling their story. Irma shushed them to silence, and put her head into the driver's side window. "Butts? Are you all right? You don't look well." He didn't. Jimmy hadn't noticed, but Butts' face was as gray as his hair.

"I'm okay, Irma, just tired from all the excitement," he mumbled, forcing a smile to his lips.

"Butts hit a home run!" Hal bellowed.

"A home run, Mr. Wagner?" Irma smiled. "Why, I didn't even know you were going to play! No wonder you look tired. Will you come in and have some breakfast?"

Butts shook his head. "No, thanks, Irma. I've got things to do. I'd like to get this truck back to Mr. Van Dorp, and I'll see about these orders." He pulled the envelope from his pocket.

"The Pirates are gonna pay me one dollar and twenty-five cents for each of the bats. We'll ship this set out to 'em next month, with the rest. They've ordered up two dozen sets at the same price! That's nearly two thousand dollars. An' I expect we'll see ten times this many orders within a month. Irma, we're in business! By this time next month, I should be able to pay all the wages and get a good start on settling my account with Mr. Hogg."

"Mr. Wagner, congratulations." Irma bent into the cab of the truck and planted a kiss on Butts' cheek. "We're all very proud of you. I'm not sure how many of the women will be able to find time to keep working, but I'm sure we can find enough folks around here to make the Wagner Baseball Equipment Company a great success. Now, you get home and get some sleep!"

Butts nodded and started up the truck. He swung it around and disappeared down the road in the direction of the Van Dorp farm.

At suppertime that evening, Irma came up to the boys' room and found them both fast asleep. She gave Jimmy a gentle shake and his eyes popped open. Her face was all red, and she looked as though she'd been crying.

"What's the matter?" Jimmy felt sick to his stomach. He knew something was wrong. He thought maybe something was the matter with his father. She bent over and gave Jimmy a big hug, and he could feel her warm tears on his neck.

"What's the matter?" he asked again.

"Jim, I want you to take a deep breath. I'm afraid I've got some bad news." Jimmy looked past her as his father slipped into the room.

"Dad," he called out to his father, "what's the matter?"

"It's bad, son," was all Wil could manage to say.

"Jim, before we wake up Hal, I want you to know. It's Butts." She bit her lip and more tears dripped down her face. His father was crying too.

"Mr. Wagner died this morning, Jim."

The words seemed all jumbled up. He understood all the words, but they didn't make sense. "He what?" Jimmy couldn't believe he'd heard it right. He looked at his father, and saw tears rolling down his cheeks. Wil stepped up to the bed and took Jimmy's hand.

"He died early this morning, just after he left here. They found him in the truck outside the Van Dorp's place. It was a heart attack, son. He probably never knew what hit him." Jimmy's father's voice was cracking.

"Butts? Butts is dead?" Nobody Jimmy knew had ever died before. He knew what dying was, but he never thought that it would happen to anybody he knew. Before he could even think about it, he was crying. Tears burned his eyes, and his throat got all sore. He thought he was going to throw up.

He jumped off his bed and ran past his parents and out of his room. He didn't stop running until he got to Butts' barn. It was all locked up. He banged on the doors and called out.

"Butts! Come on, Butts, open up! We've got bats to make! Come on!" He banged and thumped on the door, but nobody came. For a few minutes, he sat on the dirt at home plate, crying and trying not to believe what his parents had said. Butts couldn't be dead — they had too much work to do. They had to revolutionize baseball. They had an order to fill!

He ran to the back door of the house. The door was unlocked, and he walked through the rooms. There was no furniture, just wooden cartons and rolls of leather piled from floor to ceiling. He had never been into the house before. He went upstairs and slunk from room to room, hoping to find something to prove that Butts was still here.

The front bedroom was completely empty, and the blinds were shut tight. Jimmy sat down on the floor, weeping. "Butts! You can't die! We were just getting started... You can't just quit! Not now!"

From the corner of his eye, he saw a sliver of yellow light. He got up to look. There, in the back of the closet wall, was a small crack of light just up from the baseboard. As he looked more closely, Jimmy could see that there was the slightest outline of a square cut into the wall. It looked like Butts' handiwork.

There was no handle on the door, only a slit along the bottom, and Jimmy knew how it would work. He could slide the blade of his jackknife along the slit and flip the latch. That's the way Butts did things. The latch sprang with a quiet click and the door flipped open. He poked in his head and looked down a long shaft. He could see a ladder going down. He swung around, sent his legs through the hole in the wall and climbed in.

As he climbed down, the dark closed in above him, and the light below scattered longer and longer shadows on the close walls of the tunnel. Any other time the shadows alone would have scared him witless, but now Jimmy felt no fear.

He could soon see where the light came from. It was an ordinary kerosene lantern. Hung on a nail near the bottom of the shaft, it filled up the small space with bright orange light. "But who lit it?" he wondered, "and why?" He took the lantern from the nail and held it up by his shoulder, examining the room. It smelled like Butts down here too. It was clammy, and smelled like dirt, but it smelled like Butts somehow, too.

Jimmy knew he was dead. He didn't really think the old man was down here, or in the barn, or anywhere else. He could feel that Butts wasn't here anymore. But he didn't want to give him up yet. He wanted it to go on. To make bats and learn to be a ball player and have Hal's picture on a card. This was the *beginning* of an adventure. Butts wasn't supposed to die!

The lighted tunnel seemed to go off in all directions. Most of the tunnel was packed earth with bracing beams across the top. He figured he knew which way was which. Left would be toward the road, maybe out to the creek. Right would be the barn. He headed to the right, under the house, toward the barn.

At the end of the tunnel he found a long ladder leading up a dark shaft. At the top, he found one of Butts' triplatch doors and he swung up into the barn. "That's how you got into the house!" he cried.

Yesterday this stuff was the greatest collection of contraptions and gadgets ever invented. Today, it all looked different. It all looked dead. He pushed the long plank out from behind the side door and swung it wide open, filling the barn with sunshine. "Butts?" he called up to the rafters. "Are you up there?" He knew that Butts wasn't up there, but he couldn't help himself from calling out anyway.

"Come on, Butts, we're gonna revolutionize baseball!" He grabbed the red accelerator handle. "I can't do this myself, Butts." Jimmy wished with all his breaking heart that Butts would come back to finish the dream. "I need you! *baseball* needs you! You've got to come back and do it, Butts!" He shoved the accelerator into the slot. The machine jerked and roared and grumbled to life.

BAARRAAP! ZIGGAAP! HUNK HUNK HUNK BAAR-RAP! He flipped through the woodpile, looking for a really good piece of lumber. He wanted the best one.

He was going to make one last bat for Butts. He adjusted the chosen piece of ash in the claw arm and twisted the crank on the side of the machine. He wanted the bat to have distance. A home run bat. The taper would be long and thin, and the sweet spot set high. This was the hardest part. If he didn't get it just right the track would jam up. Butts would have got it right on the first try, but Jimmy got it stuck on the first row.

He skipped to the side of the machine and pulled the jackknife from his back pocket. The clattering and swooping of the claw arms didn't bother him. Jimmy had seen them in action enough to know how to avoid them. You had to be careful, but if you paid attention, there wasn't any danger. He ducked into the wild fray of elbow joints and pincer arms and set to work poking the wood free from the track. Dimly, through the roar and chatter of the machine, he thought he heard his name. "Jimmy!" He turned his head to see Hal, running in through the open door. "What are you doing?" Hal shouted.

"Hal, he's not here anymore. I'm making one last bat for him." He could see that Hal was crying hard, and he started up crying again. Through his tears, he couldn't see that the wood had come free. With a jerk, the claw arm swung loose and headed straight for him. "Hal, Butts isn't coming back, it's just you and me, now." Hal's eyes bugged out of their sockets. He could see what was coming.

The swinging claw arm caught Jimmy on the back of the head, sending him sprawling into a swirl of sawdust. Faces and strange voices tumbled around in his head. A thin boy with a brown face glared in at him and shook his head. Strange music blared from every direction at once. From out of the spinning madness, he heard someone call his name.

"**M**att! Wake up! Who's not coming back where? Wow, are you okay? Man, you're gonna have some kind of lump back there. How long have you been out here?" He didn't recognize the voice. He thought for a minute it was Hal, and he rubbed his head.

"Come on, Matt, are you okay?" said the voice. "What's all this mumbo jumbo about not coming back? Who's not coming back? And did you say you hurt your butt?"

All he could think of was how hot he was. His heart was pumping hard, and he was covered in sweat.

"Sanji?" he sputtered. The name popped out, and he knew it belonged to this voice. He spit a mouthful of grit into the hard-packed dirt. It was coming back to him. He had pulled the lever on the machine, and it had started swinging its arms around. One of them must have hit him. He rubbed his head and took the brown hand which was reaching down to him. Sanji helped him up to his knees. He could remember nothing but hitting the ground, and something about Hal. "Yea, I guess I'm okay, Sanj. Man, have I had a dream! I don't know what it was about, but it was something!"

18

Jimmy Fox

"**S**o what d'you do to get this thing goin'? It doesn't look as though it's run in fifty years, Matt. Look," the boy looked doubtfully at him, "this motor is completely rusted out!" Sanji was inspecting the motor and the levers at the end of the rolling table. "There's not even any gas in it. Are you sure it was the machine that hit you?"

"Oh, yeah," Matt said, rubbing his head. "I'm sure. I just pulled the red lever back, and the whole thing started humpin' and roarin'! I've got the goose egg to prove it."

"Anyway, if you turned it on, who turned it off? It doesn't make sense." Sanji walked along the length of the machine, shaking his head and running the palm of his hands along the rusty rollers. Matt was leaning on the side of the cast iron enigma, still rubbing his head, looking sort of dazed. Sanji continued, "You say you came in here this morning, and this happened before lunch? Man, you must have been out cold for hours!"

"Look, Sanji, I'm not feeling so hot. I think I better go in and lie down for a bit. And I don't want you sayin' anything to my mom. There's a few things I want to find out before she freaks out, okay?"

"If you say so..." Sanji was still shaking his head as the two boys walked toward the house in the late afternoon sunshine .

"It's a jolly good thing I came back with your mom. Otherwise *she'd* have found you! Anyway, she'll be back in a few minutes. She's gone to the Trading Post to see Costa. She says he's feeling pretty low. The Trading Post is up for sale!"

"Yeah, I know. Can you believe it? Costa was here this morning. He says they're going to open a McDonalds. Fergus doesn't need a hamburger joint, it'd never be like the Trading Post! Where else can you still get a Ginsue knife, or Boxcar Willie's greatest hits on eight track cassettes?" They both snickered about the eight track tapes in the back room. "And remember the garage sale? The one he was going to give us fifty bucks for? We're not going to have it. I had him talked into fifty bucks each and ten percent of the profits."

"Fifty bucks? Wow, good work. And ten percent?" Sanji added it up quickly, dreaming of a skateboard Costa had for eighty dollars. "Each?"

"Nice try, Sanji. I tried that on him, but he wouldn't go for it. Costa's a soft touch, but he's not stupid." Sanji lifted an eyebrow and made a face. "Okay," Matt agreed, "But he's not *that* stupid. Anyway, I don't think there's two hundred thousand dollars' worth of junk back there, and that's how much the building costs. So I don't think there's much chance of saving the store that way." Matt plunked down on the green sofa in the living room. Sanji stopped in the kitchen to get two tall glasses of milk from the fridge.

Matt pulled off his shoes, gulped down the milk, and lay back on the couch. "There's something very strange about that barn, Sanji. It feels weird. Especially that machine. What d'you figure it's for? It really was running you know. I didn't dream it. The dials were moving, and those rollers were spinnin'..." He rubbed the back of his head, "And the arms were moving faster than me!" He fluffed up the pillow, jabbed it under his head and closed his eyes. Sanji went for a refill, and when he came back, Matt was fast asleep, snoring quietly.

In his dream, he was back in the barn. He looked up to the platform where the sofa and tables were, expecting to see someone. There was something swinging from one side of the barn to the other.

He followed the movement across to the far side. There he was!

A tall boy in blue overalls stood at the edge of the platform, pointing towards the windows. He was very high up, but Matt could tell that the boy was excited about something. His other hand held a lantern, which he swung back and forth in the beams of late afternoon sun. Suddenly Matt knew the boy's name, and he was calling up to him. He was shouting, but no sound was coming out of his mouth.

"Jimmy who?" It was Costa's voice. "Hey, Matt, are you gonna sleep all day, or do you want some pizza?" Costa was waving a slice of steaming pepperoni and pineapple pizza under his nose. "I knew you couldn't sleep through pizza, nephew." He set the plate down on the coffee table. "Who's Jimmy?"

"Jimmy Fox." Matt didn't know why he said it. The name just jumped out of his mouth. He bit his tongue and stared at the pizza. He was still half asleep.

"Who's Jimmy Fox?" Costa continued.

"I don't know who Jimmy Fox is, what's it to you?" he snapped at his uncle.

"Well you were calling his name in your sleep, okay? People don't usually dream about people they don't know, do they, smart guy?"

"It's just the name that came to mind when you asked me who Jimmy was! What is this?" he barked. He was ticked off at Costa, but he wasn't sure why. "Am I on trial? I just said it, okay. I don't know anybody named Jimmy Fox."

"Okay, okay," Costa laughed, "I just asked. Sheesh. Touchy, eh? Maria!" He called out to Matt's mother in the kitchen, "Can you bring the whole box out here? I think your son needs food. He's grouchy as a bear!"

Sanji emerged from the kitchen with the pizza box in one hand, and a slice on a plate in the other. "Oh, he's grouchy all right, Costa, he had a fight with reality today. And he lost. Check out the goose egg on his head."

"Shut-up, Sanji!" Matt hissed.

"Let's see, Matt." Costa put his chubby hand on the back of Matt's head. He felt the knobby lump which had puffed up from the blow. "Ooh, I'll bet that smarts, nephew. Somebody catch you from behind?"

"It's okay," he lied, "it's nothing. It doesn't even hurt." Matt wanted to change the subject, fast. "Look, Costa, just shut up about it, okay. I don't want my mom to know anything about it. I'm all right, but I don't want her going off on a freak-out. I'll tell you about it later."

"Okay, little big man, but I'm gonna hang around tonight. That's the deal. I'll keep my mouth shut, but I'm staying out here tonight to keep an eye on you. A smack in the head can be serious." He frowned, then smiled.

"The best thing for a smack in the head is another piece of pizza and a ballgame. Jays and Boston at seven thirty-five. In fact," Costa squinted at his watch, "we can probably catch the pre-game show right about now."

When Maria found them, they had the television and the radio going at the same time. The Jays were down a run, fielding in the third, and she had the reinforcements. She waved the bag of Oreos around the room, letting each of the boys dip in for a couple. "Don't I even get a hello? Three creeps." She swept wisps of fuzzy black hair away from her eyes and sneered at them.

They said "Hi, mom", "Yo, Mrs. Zonjic", and "Yeah, sorry Sis," in turn and she set the bag of cookies on the coffee table.

"So what'd you do today?" she asked, looking past Costa to where Matt was sprawled on the couch.

The voice on the radio was very excited. "It's going... going... It's gone! Home run, Jimmy Fox!" and Matt's fresh slice of pizza hit the floor. Costa turned to him, laughing, "That's your guy! Jimmy Fox, Matt... You were dreaming about the Boston Red Sox! *Matt?*" Matt was out cold.

19

Moonlight

Matt woke up in his bed. Moonbeams bathed his room in a pale yellow glow, and cast shadows on the walls all around him. A cool, wet cloth was draped over his forehead and he wiped it down across his face. He sat up slowly and looked around his room. Sanji was sleeping soundly in the other bed. He reached for the glass of water on the window sill, and took a long sip. He felt completely awake, refreshed.

He climbed to his knees on the bed and looked out the window. The moon, high over the fields, was broad and yellow. The barn cast a short, dark moon-shadow across the field. His eye caught something at the edge of the shadow, and he looked again. From up here, in this strange light, it almost looked as though a baseball diamond was sketched into the grass. The grass was thicker where bases would be, and the ground was completely flat, except where it rose up softly toward a perfect pitcher's mound. He could almost make out baselines, and a home plate. The barn could be a backstop. It stood about twenty feet behind the plate, dead square to the field.

Matt rubbed his eyes, erasing the baseball diamond from his imagination. He sat back down on the bed, and drank the rest of the water. There was something else too, though. He knelt up again and gazed into the night. There was a light on in the barn! When he had looked at the barn before, he hadn't really noticed it. It was just a faint orange glow around the front doors and a soft flicker licking the grass at the doorway.

Matt looked over at his sleeping friend. When Sanji went to sleep, he stayed asleep. There was no point in trying to wake him up. Matt crept silently out of his room and down the stairs.

Costa was snoring softly on the couch. Matt swept past him, and quietly swung the back door open.

The night rang with the rhythm of the country symphony. Crickets set up the back beat, while night birds and frogs chattered their endless melody. Matt stood amazed at the racket. He wondered how anybody could sleep through all this noise. He padded over to where he'd seen the baseball diamond. It was a perfectly flat field, and although a lot of it was garden, it was about the right size for a diamond. But how could it be? He decided it wasn't a baseball diamond at all. Not yet, he mumbled to himself.

He turned back to the barn. There *was* a sort of light inside. He had closed the place up properly before supper, and he couldn't imagine his mother going out there. Sanji was asleep upstairs, Costa was on the couch, so who could be out here?

The door wasn't latched, and he swung it gently back, just enough to squeak through. He stood beside the door, his back to the wall, and looked into the enormous room. Moonlight streamed in through the upper windows, giving the lofts a speckled yellow wash. Matt slipped through the doorway and into the semi-dark of the barn.

The dim glow from a lantern in the machine room cast tall jagged shadows up along the walls. Claw arms sent long, spidery silhouettes dancing among the cobwebs and cracks. Something moved among the flittering shadows.

A leathery voice broke the hollow silence. "Well, I'll be..." Matt nearly jumped out of his skin. "I got me a moonlight visitor."

A figure moved, shadowless, across the floor. He wore a black overall and his long, ruddy face showed beneath a fringe of gray hair. He had a strangely familiar smile.

"Can he see me?" the old man muttered to himself. "Naw... He can't see me." The man spun a toothpick around in his mouth and grinned a big, white-toothed grin. He pulled his chin and spit the toothpick into the dirt. It landed about three feet out from his shoes, straight up and firmly planted.

He couldn't do that again in a hundred years! Matt thought to himself. If this was a dream, it was a doozie. The light was eerie; things seemed to glow, even the air was somehow strange; it was sweet, like sawdust and leather. It all seemed so real. Almost real, he thought to himself. He wondered if you could faint in a dream. Matt crouched closer to the wall.

"Well, I'll be the ghost of Abraham Lincoln! He can see me! You took some powerful whop t'yer walnut, boy," the man continued. "Yer okay, though, ain'tcha?" Matt said nothing from his hide among the shadows. "I've seen funny things happen to people who mess with that machine..."

The old man grinned into the dark barn. "Keepin' your lip buttoned, eh? Okay, then. I'll do the talkin'." He pursed his lips and took Matt's silence as agreement.

"Let's talk about baseball. Baseball's my game," he said, matter-of-factly, "I know a bit about how it all works, you see..." He was quiet for a short moment, pausing to spit another toothpick into the dirt.

"It's all I really know about, I suppose...and its all memories now anyway." A new toothpick appeared in his mouth and slid to the corner of his smile. "Memories are..." his eyes drifted upward into the high reaches of the gigantic barn. "Memories are important. And dreams. They're the same sort of things, ya know, dreams and memories." He looked sharply toward Matt and said excitedly, "You see, neither of them are real except while you have 'em, and when they're over, or you forget 'em, why..." his hand passed over his eyes and away, "they're gone!"

"So where'd they go?" The man scratched his head and looked as though the question made sense to him. "Are they in your head? Well, they weren't always in your head, were they? So where were they before they were in your head? Where were they before they happened? Or later? It gets pretty complicated, don't it?" Matt watched and listened as if in a trance. The man's silver hair shimmered like a wispy halo over his broad, ruddy face. His wild eyes flashed orange and black with the light and shadow. "Life is complicated. And unpredictable." The man reached into the side pocket of his baggy overalls. He pulled out a handkerchief and gave his nose a tug.

At the same moment, Matt reached into his own pocket. He jumped as his fingers closed around a jackknife. A jackknife he'd never seen before. The man held his head between the palms of his hands, and spun around to look at the boy. The light flickered and for a minute, Matt couldn't see him.

"The knife! You've got the knife! Haven'tcha?" The voice sounded far away. "How'd you get it? Just put it away!" Startled at the sharp tone, Matt thrust the knife back into his pocket.

The light flickered to bright again. He could see the man more clearly, now, standing on the far side of the machine, looking along the floor as if he had lost something.

"Anyway, anyway, anyway, so here we are. That knife is gonna cause problems, though, I guarantee it. Can't figure how you came to have it. Doesn't make sense." Matt understood almost none of this. Finding the jackknife had given him a tingling feeling up his spine. Who was this old man, and what was he talking about?

The man folded his arms over his chest and closed one of his sparkling eyes. He looked up at the rafters and then back to the silent boy in the shadows.

"Did you ever play baseball, at least?" he asked hopefully.

"Some," Matt said suddenly, from the dark. This, at least, was something familiar.

"Well, good. That's good. So you're a baseball man?"

"Well," Matt said, a little louder. "I know a little about it..."

"Well are you a baseball man or not?" he barked. "If you are a baseball man, you may as well come on out of that dark corner and make the acquaintance of another one!" The man's hands rested on his hips, and he grimaced into the shadows. "I'm gettin' tired of talkin' to somebody I can't even see! It's like I'm talkin' to a *ghost* or somethin'."

Matt stepped into the broad circle of lamplight and felt for the

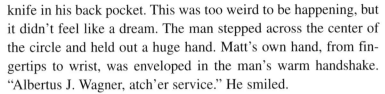

knife in his back pocket. This was too weird to be happening, but it didn't feel like a dream. The man stepped across the center of the circle and held out a huge hand. Matt's own hand, from fingertips to wrist, was enveloped in the man's warm handshake. "Albertus J. Wagner, atch'er service." He smiled.

"Matt Killburn," Matt stammered, "I, I live here. What are you doing in my barn in the middle of the night, mister, ah, Wagner?" he asked cautiously.

Wagner paid no attention to the question. "Glad to know you, Matthew and please, call me Butts. You see, I already know who you are. I mean, I've seen you 'round here, picking locks and goin' where you don't necessarily belong... I watch over my stuff, you know. Always have." The old man had a new toothpick going, and he waltzed toward a crate and leaned against it. "They've cleared a lot of it out over the years, but I've still got everything I need. I've always looked after things here."

Matt looked up to the loft high above them. He remembered that there was a rocking chair up there with the initials A.W. carved in the back of it. Albertus Wagner? The name Butts Wagner was vaguely familiar, but right now he couldn't think why. "You live here?" he sputtered. "You're A.W. from the loft? You live here?"

"Well," the old man nodded, "in a sort of a way, yes. I guess you might say I come with the territory. But don't worry, I don't ever bother anybody." He spit the toothpick into the dirt where it stood half an inch from the one before, end up in the hard dirt floor. "Just so long as they leave my stuff alone," he chuckled.

"Leave your stuff alone?" Matt stammered.

"I had a renter once, in the house, wanted to burn all the lumber I've got stashed in the far loft." He waved his arm loosely in the direction of the far loft. "I didn't keep all that ash wood for some good-for-nothin' louse to burn in a bonfire. So I put him into a squeeze play... Fixed him good!" Wagner slapped his knee and snorted. "I'm afraid I might have been a bit hard on him. I heard tell he wound up in a mental institution." He chuckled quietly to himself, and suddenly looked across to Matt.

"Now, I didn't make him crazy, he was crazy when he got here.

I just recognized it and exploited it." Wagner explained, "A mental institution's a good place for a guy who'd burn the finest collection of lumber ever assembled for mass production. Wouldn't you say, Matthew?"

"Ah..." Matt was speechless. He had no idea what the man was talking about. "Sure..." he ventured.

"And there was Mrs. Dalton. She owned the place then. She was the one who destroyed the diamond... Planted gladiolas in center field. Gladiolas! Seeded the baselines and took out the benches! *Burned* the benches!" he hollered. "The most perfect ball yard in the known world, and she plants gladiolas in center field. Women!" He paced across the circle of light, spun on his heel, and continued, jabbing his finger in Matt's direction.

"I tried everything to make her leave things alone. I got her to stop burning stuff for firewood, but when she decided to take down the barn, I had to act. I had to do it!"

"You had to do what?" Matt whispered. He was beginning to wonder if this man wasn't crazy, and maybe dangerous. He felt his back pocket again for the knife. He wasn't sure why.

"Well for heaven's sake, Matthew. I wouldn't do anything to hurt anyone. But I sure scared the heck out of her! I put on a show like you wouldn't believe! Gave her the full treatment." He laughed, "Why, when I got done with her, the real estate agents for miles around wouldn't come near the place!" He chuckled. "I was all by myself here for years."

His toothpick spun around, ragged end out this time, and he continued as if he had known Matt Killburn all his life. "And then there was the McGinty years."

"The McGintys had four marvelous, stupid, hulking boys, who played ball like they were born for nothin' but playin' ball. The youngest, Alistair McGinty — gadzooks! He was about the strongest and dimmest young man I've ever seen play the game. He could hit the ball a ton! Couldn't hit a real pitcher, I'll wager, he was way too stupid, but my, my, my, what he couldn't have done with one of my 6-11-24s. If he'd only had the imagination to listen to me, well..." He wiped his enormous hands across his chest, bringing them to a halt on his hips. "But he didn't."

Matt wondered what a 6-11-24 might be. "Did all these people agree to let you live in the barn?" Matt wondered out loud. "Did they, ah, rent you the place, or something?" He was shivering a little, he noticed. "Do my mother and uncle know you live here?"

The words sounded hollow even as Matt said them. He knew there was something wrong here. Albertus Wagner was a name from the encyclopedia. It came to him suddenly. Butts Wagner. Washington and New York, sometime before 1900. Eighteen ninety-something. If this was the Butts Wagner he'd be over a hundred years old! And this guy didn't look a day over sixty!

The toothpick, now ragged on both ends, spun end over end and landed softly on top of two already standing in the dirt, a bridge over two pillars. Matt was convinced now, that he would wake up in his bed, very soon, and laugh about all this tomorrow.

There was something else about the man's name. Wagner. It was the name on the barrel of Costa's bat! The Wagner Baseball Equipment Company. Did he dream the bat, too? Suddenly he knew the initials on the butt of the bat stood for Jimmy Fox. Why did he know that name? There was a Jimmy Fox who played for Boston this year, and there was Jimmy Foxx, 'Double X' he was called, but it wasn't those Jimmy Foxes... He looked from the toothpick-bridge up to the grinning man who hadn't answered his questions. "How long," he asked, feebly, "have you been living here?"

"Matthew," Butts Wagner perched his bottom on the crate, bent into the light and caught Matt's stare at eye level. "I haven't lived here in more than sixty years. But I've been here since 1928. You don't get it, do ya?" He closed one eye and squinted over at the boy. "Do I have to spell it out for ya?" The man jumped to his feet and jiggled his arms in the air. "Boo! Bah! Boo! I'm a ghost!" he laughed.

He dropped his arms and pointed to the ground. "I died, right here in Wellington County, in the year nineteen hundred and twenty-eight. I'm in the books. You can look it up!"

Matt felt the hairs on his neck standing on end. He was suddenly terrified, but he spoke in spite of his fear. "You don't look much like a ghost..."

Wagner folded his arms over his chest and leaned back. "I could disappear for ya or something. How about if I float around the barn..." He squinted at the doubtful boy and cocked his head.

"Naw. You don't seem to care whether I'm man or ghost. Maybe young fellows today don't feel connected to earthly reality like we did, what with all the movin' pictures you watch on those boxes in the house. Maybe you figure they're just as real as I am. But we don't need to dwell on our different relations to reality, do we?" Matt said nothing. "Well, do we, boy?"

"How do I know? I don't even know what you said!" Matt cried, "Besides, I don't believe in ghosts. There's no such thing." Matt was feeling bolder now. The guy was crazy, after all. "Are you related to the Wagner of the Wagner Baseball Equipment Company?"

Butts rose up off of the crate and strutted across to the machine. He put his huge hands on the edge, and rubbed it gently, his back to the boy. "The baseball company? This, Matthew," he waved his hand at the machine, "is about all that's left of the Wagner Baseball Equipment Company."

"This, and what lumber and other hardgoods I've managed to scare people away from. Yes, I am the Wagner Baseball Equipment Company. Manufacturer of the Wagner Whacker. The finest baseball bat ever used between the white lines. Ever heard of it?" He turned his head to the side, then looked back at his machine, as if trying to remember something. "Naw, you wouldn't have heard of the Whacker."

"Heard of it?" Matt grinned. This was better than TV. "Sure I've heard of it. I've got one!"

The man spun around and stared at the boy. The look on his face was so hard and real that Matt had no more doubts. This was real. "You've got one? You've got a Whacker?" he snapped. "Then you know! You know!

"You've hit with it? Matthew, if you've hit with it, then you must know!"

"I, I," Matt stuttered, embarrassed that he'd never even so much as swiped fresh air with it, "It looks like it could drive a sinker over the wall..." he muttered, feeling a little foolish about not taking the bat seriously.

"A sinker, eh? I suppose that's one of them new fangled pitches that don't spin? I never had the pleasure of hitting one of them." A new toothpick came from nowhere and danced on his lips. "Satchel Paige threw that kind of fancy, carnival stuff. Nobody else did. And in more tries than I care to remember, I never got a hit off Satchel Paige."

"You batted against Satchel Paige?" Matt chuckled. "Why not? Nothing else here is making any sense. You're a ghost and you played against Satchel Paige. Why not?"

"*And* Christie Matthewson with his famous fade away. Matthewson was the only one to ever come close to Paige in speed." Wagner blinked over at Matt. "Let's get back to your Whacker. There aren't any, so far as I know. All the ones we took down to Watertown were burned up by Mrs. Dalton. But that's another story. Maybe a few found their way into team equipment bags and players' private collections. My brother Honus had a few — souvenirs of the Watertown marathon," he winked, as if Matt should understand what he was talking about, "but you wouldn't have one o' *them*, would ya?"

"No," Matt answered, truthfully. "Your brother was Honus Wagner? Honus Wagner the greatest infielder to ever play the game?" Matt Killburn knew just about everything there was to know about Honus 'Dutchie' Wagner, holder of more records than any man of his time.

"The very same. I believe Honnie is out playing baseball in a cornfield in Iowa, but that's another story too." Matt didn't ask what he meant. Only half of what the old man made sense, and that half was unbelievable anyway.

"He's a ghost, too, of course." Matt laughed. "We could ask him what he did with his Whackers. Maybe he's playing with Ty Cobb!"

Ol' Man Wagner looked sharply at Matt and sucked air into his puckered lips. "Ty Cobb?" He shook his head. "I don't like to speak ill of the dead, Matthew, but Ty Cobb was a weed, a blemish on the record books. He thrived in a world of gentlemen because he didn't play it fair. Ty Cobb was a bad apple. If my brother is playing ball with Ty Cobb for eternity, then there is no justice in the universe!"

"But tell me about your Wagner Whacker. A guy who owns a Wagner Whacker and never got a hit with it..." He shook his head in disbelief. "Well, is it a line drive bat or a long ball hitter?"

"I, I think it's a long ball hitter. It belonged to somebody named J.F. His initials are carved into the end..."

20

Something Lost

"Jimmy Fox!" the old man roared. "James' bat! The Original Wagner Whacker!" His jaws shut tight. He was speechless. His mouth began to move silently and his head wagged from side to side. Matt found this all too familiar. It was something about the dreams he'd been having. Something about Jimmy Fox, and the machine, and the light in the old man's eyes. He'd seen all this before. Somehow.

"James's own Whacker!" he whistled, "Why, I'd forgotten. James got the first one we ever made. A Letters-Up-Line-Drive-Hitter! A classic. Why, I saw a washed-up hitter from Cincinnati poke a clothesline that ripped clear through the crowd in center field with that bat. Would'a gone four hundred feet if it hadn't hit somebody... I don't suppose he ever used it again, after his accident."

"His accident?" Matt asked.

"Oh yes. Poor James was never the same after the accident. He was knocked out cold by my contraption here. He was hurt pretty bad, too. I kept an eye on him, but under the circumstances, I wasn't much help to anybody."

"The circumstances?" Matt asked.

"Yes, you see, James couldn't see me. I was always here, but he couldn't see me the way you can."

"Some people can see a ghost, and some can't. There's no explaining it, that's just the way it is. Oh," Butts spun the rollers

143

on the machine, and nodded, smiling, "I mean, a ghost can scare almost anybody, if he's any sort of ghost, but you can't make people see you. Some people can, and some can't. James couldn't."

Matt wanted to say that the reason he could see him was because he wasn't a ghost! There's no such thing as ghosts. But he said nothing, because he wanted to hear about Jimmy Fox. He knew the name as well as he knew his own.

"He told Hazel McPherson in here one night... They sat here, much like we're sittin' here, only he had his arm around her... He told her that when he was out cold, he dreamed that a boy would find something in here." Wagner's head bobbed around the room, considering all the possible hiding places in the vast building. "James said he'd lost it, but it was okay because the boy would find it, the boy would know exactly what to do with it. He wanted the boy to have it. James said it was a vision of the future!

"He scared poor Hazel out of her wits! And he said — what was it? Yes, that the boy would be a dreamer, too, and that he had a dream which would lead him to adventure, and glory!" His eyes blazed in the flickering light. "James said he wished I could be around to see it. So maybe he'll get his wish." He was silent for a few moments, rubbing his hands on the rough overalls.

"For many years, James would come and sit by the machine, and stare out these doors. I hoped he might just pick up where we left off. He could'a done it. Everything he needed was here! We had lumber, leather, tools and paint, everything you might need to manufacture baseball equipment. But he never did." Matt pictured Jimmy Fox, looking out the door, seeing these same stars, breathing this sweet air, and wondering how any of this made sense.

"One day," the big man snickered, "James just grew up. Married Hazel McPherson. Even then he came back from time to time, but I could never get through to him. Tried everything. Some people know I'm here the minute they step onto the farm, and others, like James, are too practical. Their brain sort of filters out what it doesn't believe in.

"Are you a dreamer, Matthew?" Butts looked hopefully across the circle of light. "I guess you must be, otherwise you wouldn't be able to see me." He was quiet for a minute, then he spoke again. "My dream was to do something great for baseball; and I nearly did it! I came *that* close." He held his finger and thumb a hair's width apart. "And then, well, I don't know what happened. One minute I was alive, more alive than I had ever been, and the next minute, everything was different. I was," he wagged his head as though he wasn't sure what the word was. "I was, well, dead."

"Heart attack. I never expected it to happen, but then, nobody does. Do you follow me, Matthew?" His bright eyes burned in on Matt's face.

Matt thought about it. He thought he understood what the man was saying, but he'd never really thought about anything like this before. He never even believed in ghosts before. He didn't really believe in them now, but why *couldn't* this Wagner be a ghost? It was almost comforting to believe it.

"Sort of," he answered. "Does everybody just hang around when they die?" Matt was thinking of his father now, wondering if somehow his dad was watching him. Maybe he was here all the time, only Matt didn't have the imagination to see him.

"No, Matthew. I don't think so. Just those of us with unfinished business." Butts Wagner's face twisted into a painful grin. "Just those of us who weren't satisfied. Those who can't rest." He flipped a toothpick into his mouth and pulled his hand down over his face, as if he were trying to wipe the pain away. "I'm tired. Sixty years is a long time, even for a ghost.

"This place just won't let me go. I guess I just won't rest 'til my job is done."

"What job?" Matt asked. He was almost afraid to hear the answer.

"The job?" The old man laughed out loud. "What's the job? Why, to finish what we started! To pass along the knowledge gained over a lifetime of careful study of the greatest game ever invented! The job, Matthew, is to revolutionize the game of baseball!" The man sprang back to life. "Nothing less than that."

"Since the time I was old enough to think, I've watched men play baseball. I've studied the relationship between muscle, wood and leather all my life. And I know how to make them work together effectively. Scientifically. Why, take Honus for example. I taught the boy everything he knew. And what did he become?" Matt was on the verge of saying 'a shortstop', when Butts Wagner answered his own question. "He became the greatest player of his day. Maybe of any day."

"Baseball is a hitting game, as you know," he winked. "And the secret to hitting a baseball is to transfer all the energy to the ball. Energy transfer. It's the principle involved in throwing, and it's the principle behind the Wagner Whacker. The Wagner Whacker is a baseball bat designed and perfected under the most rigorous conditions. The relationship between the length, girth and relative weight that effects the release of the energy as transferred from the batter, the ball, and the pitcher determines the type of hit you can expect. This is *science*, Matthew. The science of *baseball*!"

Matt was swept up in the fire of the old man's eyes, and in the idea of perfecting the game he loved.

"This machine, Matthew," he began, spinning the glittering silver rollers. They whirred like the flutter of a pheasant in the brush. "This machine and that old bat hold the secrets of a lifetime of study. The notes and figuring are all up there," he nodded toward the loft. "Blueprints for the design and manufacture of the greatest baseball equipment ever imagined. Volumes of information. It's all still there, over on the far side. The job is to bring those principles into practice. To bring science to the ball park."

"What else did Jimmy say about the boy in his dream?" The flutter of the rollers was like the smell of fresh-baked cookies: they reminded him of something. They reminded him of ice cold Coca-Cola, and of the smell of fresh sawdust. And he began to remember things about Jimmy Fox.

After all, he thought to himself, I do have the knife. He looked to where he had first seen it, hanging on a nail near the door. And I have the bat. I am the boy, he thought, but he didn't say so to Wagner, yet. "What would the boy find?" he asked instead.

"Now, that's interesting. I never understood it myself. He told Hazel, oh, two or three times, that the boy would find something that James had lost. And that it would have made me so happy." The old man spit his toothpick into the dirt, adding to the small forest of upright picks already in place.

"Could it be the bat? The Wagner Whacker?"

"Naw. Not a chance. That bat ain't been in this barn since the day it was made. You think I wouldn't have seen it here over the last sixty years? Mind you I am happy you've got it. Even if you never got a hit with it. That bat belongs here, with all this other stuff. But it wasn't the bat."

"The knife!" Matt whistled. "It's the knife!" He pulled the knife from his pocket. It was about eight inches long and was faced on either side with smooth bone. He rubbed it with his thumb, and flipped it open with his other hand. The blade glistened orange in the odd light.

The man's pained grin suddenly sank. "No, it's not the knife." He seemed to be fading. Matt could see the glistening machine right through him. His voice seemed to come from nowhere.

"Jimmy had the knife when he was knocked over by the right centerman pivot here." He touched the middle claw arm. The same one that had snuck up on Matt. "It was in his hand when he went down, but when he got up, that old knife was gone. That knife left this barn the day Jimmy had his accident. How you got it, I don't know, but that's not what James was referring to. And put that thing away! I don't think it's right. Just put it away!"

Matt slipped the knife back into his pocket. "Well then, what?" he demanded. "He must have been dreaming about me! It's obvious. What am I supposed to find?"

"I guess it depends," the old man bent and picked up the lantern, "on whether you are the boy in his dream. Dreams are darned strange things, you know. The rules are all different here. I suppose you'll know what it is when you find it. You do have the knife, after all, and that must mean somethin'. "

The man and light began to fade. "I don't think I can help you, Matthew. I'm afraid that's the way this works."

First the man disappeared, then the lantern stood alone in midair for a split second. With a flicker the light disappeared completely, leaving Matt in the dark, empty barn. He ran to the spot where the man had disappeared, his hands groping in the dark. The voice came from high above in the loft. "It's all in the dream, Matthew..."

His knees were shaking, and he could hear his heart pounding in his ears. With a million questions jangling in his head, and a new bruise on his elbow, he shuffled back to his bed and fell into a deep, dream-filled sleep.

21

Whack!

It was late when the sun finally got around to waking Matt. He could hear Costa downstairs in the kitchen.

"He's okay, Maria. Get a grip! It's a bump on the head, not a brain tumor!" He couldn't hear his mother's reply. "Look, I'll take him and Sanji in to the store with me. I'll keep an eye on him and I'll have them back by dinner. I could take him around to Dr. Marconi if it makes you feel better." Costa was winning. Matt knew his uncle pretty well. He knew what it sounded like when he was losing an argument with his sister, and what it sounded like when he was winning. He was definitely winning this one.

Matt reached around and felt the goose egg on his head while he was on his way to the bathroom. It wasn't too bad. It was hardly sore at all. And he felt fine.

There was definitely something different today, though. He was brushing his teeth, looking into the mirror, looking closely for signs of darker hair on his upper lip. There wasn't anything different in the mirror. It was the way he was thinking that was different.

When he came into the kitchen, Maria and Costa were discussing Costa's future. If he wasn't going to have the Trading Post anymore, he had to find some way of paying his share of the farm.

"I can go back out west," Costa said. He was waving a slice of toast, as if wafting it in the air would help him think. "They need machinists in Alberta."

Maria pinched her face and rolled her eyes.

"Okay," Costa shrugged, "there aren't as many jobs out there as there was in the old days, but, hey, a guy like me..." he pointed at himself, "they need guys like me. They've got all that old drilling equipment. It needs fixing all the time. And I can fix anything!" His hands waved as though he were trying to prove that he could fix things. "And hey, I've still got friends in Fort McMurray, no problem."

Maria shook her head. "You're not going out west, Costa. You hated working out there!" Maria took the toast from him and buttered it. "Every letter I got, all the time you were out there, was the same: Dear Sis. It's cold, dark, and..."

"And it pays me forty-eight bucks an hour to put up with it," he said, taking the toast back and biting into it. "I can buy a lotta blankets and flashlights with forty-eight bucks an hour. I can send you my half of this place every month..."

"We don't want money from my grumpy brother in Fort Godknowswhere Alberta," she moaned, "we want bad coffee and postage stamps from the Trading Post. Why can't you just rent another building and move all the stuff from the Trading Post there?" Maria couldn't understand what all the fuss was about. It seemed pretty simple to her.

"It wouldn't be the same." Costa flipped the toaster and snapped up two slices, golden brown. "The Trading Post is, well, it's my life. It wouldn't be the same if I just moved to another building. Having the Trading Post was like sinking into a warm, cozy world; I sell everything people need. So people come in from time to time and buy some of it... It's a life. And now somebody just turns off the lights, shuts off the heat and says, take a hike, we're gonna open a burger palace." His eyes were getting puffy, like he might even cry, Matt thought.

"No, Maria, it's not like I can just find another store. I've got to move on to something with some adventure. I think it's time for a big change."

"And you call going back to a punch-clock job a big change? An adventure? I call it a cop out!"

Matt couldn't stand it any more. It all sounded so stupid. He grabbed a piece of toast from Costa's plate and dropped two fresh slices into the toaster. "Maybe the McDonalds needs a manager, Costa." He imagined Costa in a little hat and uniform. It was ridiculous. "I don't think they'll let you give away free second cups of coffee, though."

Sanji called in from outside. "Hey, Matt, I've been working on a new slider with Mike Hereford." He poked his head into the kitchen. "You've got to keep your eye on it or you'll never catch it." Sanji had already had his breakfast. He'd been outside bouncing a tennis ball off the barn wall, waiting for Matt to wake up so they could explore the barn and figure out the mystery of the dead machine. "You want to see if you can catch it?"

Matt grabbed his decker and his chest protector, and headed out the back door to play some catch. "What d'ya mean, 'see if I can catch your slider'? Anything you can throw and Hereford can catch should be no problem, Mr. All-star."

Sanji stood on the raised area out beside the barn, and Matt paced out the sixty-foot-six-inch distance from the mound, laid down a spare baseball cap to mark home plate and squatted down to catch his friend's new slider. Sanji wound up and delivered a breaking ball. Matt snapped his decker around the ball and threw it back without comment. Sanji threw another and another, and Matt just tossed them back without saying anything. Finally, Sanji had to speak. "So what do you think of the new pitch?"

"It's breaking too soon. Nobody's going to swing at it, Sanj. It's breaking four feet out from the plate. Change the release point and snap it harder."

Sanji didn't mind being criticized, but he didn't like Matt's tone of voice. "Oh, sure, it's breaking too soon. I *want* it to break early. I want it to look like a fastball, so when they think they can take it downtown, the bottom just falls out of it, and whoosh, they swipe fresh air."

"Nice try Sanji." Matt was thinking that it wasn't a bad pitch, but he was mostly thinking about what had happened last night. He didn't believe, now, that it really had happened. It was a dream, like the dream about the pointing boy in the loft. "Bring the breaking point in by six inches, and maybe you've got a good pitch. Maybe." He knew this would get Sanji's goat, and for some reason, he really wanted to get Sanji mad. It worked.

Sanji wound up and fired a wild fastball over Matt's head. It hit the wall of the barn with a deafening crack, and rolled halfway back out to the pitcher's mound. Matt didn't flinch. He was still crouched behind the home plate cap, glove out over the plate, as if waiting for the pitch. "So are we out here to throw sliders, or temper tantrums? Who do you think you are, Todd Stottlemyre?" he sneered.

"You're a jerk, Killburn. I don't think I want to do either. Not here anyway. I'll save my slider for Mike Hereford. At least he makes an effort to catch them." Sanji knew that this would get to Matt. And it did.

Killburn dropped his glove and headed out to the mound. He had every intention of slugging Sanji, and he probably would have, if Costa had not come out just then, with a baseball bat slung over his shoulder.

"Hey, I'll take a piece of that slider!" he called, strutting around the side of the barn.

"You couldn't hit a basketball tossed underhand!" Matt snarled.

"Try me, you little creeps." Matt returned to his place behind the home plate cap, and slammed his fist into the pocket of the glove.

"Okay, Slugger, see if you can hit wonder boy's new slider. But you should have a golf club, not a baseball bat. He breaks so early you'll have to dig it out of the dirt to hit it."

Costa ground his feet into the grass, and swung the bat a couple of times, waiting for Sanji to begin his wind up. Matt crouched behind him, and whispered to Costa. "Don't swing where the ball is coming; swing it down around your knees. The bottom drops out and it comes across the plate around your shins. It looks like a fastball, but just wait it out and it'll break downward hard."

Sanji paused with the glove at chest level and pulled his throwing arm back. When he released the pitch, it was spinning slowly, coming in at waist level, looking for all the world like a very hittable fastball. Costa swung at it and the ball snapped into Matt's waiting glove. "Anybody for golf?" yelled Matt. He dropped to his knees and tossed the ball back to the big grin on the pitcher's mound.

He looked up at Costa and sneered. "I told you. It's not a fastball. Swing low. Don't look at where it's coming. Just swing low." The next pitch was on its way, and looked exactly like the last one. Costa swiped the bat around and missed the ball by about six inches.

"Oh, for Pete's sake, Costa," Matt grumbled into his glove, "I'm tryin' to tell you how to hit this pitch. Would you just listen to me and swing when I tell you! And swing low! One more strike and Lefty out there will think he's in line for the Cy Young award. Do us all a favor and hit the thing this time wouldja!"

Sanji wound up for the payoff, and delivered the exact same pitch. "Swing low!" Matt muttered as the pitch left Sanji's hand. Costa waited on it, and although the ball was coming in at belt level, he swung the bat down below his knees. He got all of the ball, and golfed it high and hard into the clear blue morning. Matt stood, Sanji wheeled, and Costa whistled as they watched the ball fly high over center field, into the sun. They all had to squint to follow it up, over the garden, easily four hundred feet out, and down into the long grass where they would never find it.

"Somebody get this guy a contract!" Sanji shouted. "That thing is outtahere!"

"Luckiest bat I ever came across," Costa muttered. "Mr. Defranco? You know, the guy I got this bat from? I gave him thirty bucks' worth of lottery tickets. He won half a million dollars on Thursday! Half a million. And all I got was this bat!" He hefted the bat and swung it through the air. "But what a bat!" he yelped. "And I gave the bat," he groaned, waving the bat over his head, "to my ungrateful nephew!"

"Costa," Sanji walked in from the mound. "Lemme see that thing." He took the bat and studied it carefully. Matt was dumfounded. The old man, Butts Wagner, had said that it was a Line Drive bat. That it was a Letters-Up-Line-Drive-Hitter. He took the bat from Sanji.

"The principle employed here is direct energy transfer," he said, amazed at himself. "Baseball is a hitting game. The secret to perfect hitting is to transfer all the hitter's energy from the hitter to the ball."

"What are you?" Sanji laughed, "Einstein of the ballpark?"

"Maybe," Matt muttered, his eyes never leaving the lucky object. "There's a box of balls in the shed, can you get it for me? And," he nodded to Sanji, "save up your strength, Slider, we've got an experiment to conduct." Sanji and Costa went to the barn to get the balls and Matt stood dumbstruck in the morning sun, running his fingers and his brain over the Wagner Whacker.

Sanji brought the box of balls to the mound, and Costa squatted in behind the plate, steadying himself with his free hand. "Relax, Costa, I'm not gonna miss any." He swiped the bat over the plate, waiting for Sanji's windup. The ball came in low and inside, and Matt leaned back to get all of it.

When the bat hit the ball, Matt felt himself shudder. There was no sting, not even a quiver in his fingers, as the leather and wood collided. The ball made contact at about the center point, below the fattest part, and so it sailed off between second and third. Sanji couldn't get to it, and it hovered out over the baseline, into left-center field, and came to earth as a respectable double. "Gimme a fastball, chest high," Matt barked.

The ball came in just below shoulder height, spinning like a top. Matt brought the bat across with the letters up. He knew exactly where the ball would be, and how long it took to get there. When the ball met the bat, Sanji didn't even consider trying to catch it. He saw the ball leave the bat on a track to take his head off and he fell back into the short grass.

The ball whizzed over the infield at an unbelievable speed. Nobody, no Major Leaguer, no Hall of Famer, could have gotten to that ball. It bounced in behind second and would have gotten even the slowest runner to first base. "Energy transfer," Matt laughed.

"Matt," Costa whistled, "did you have Wheaties for breakfast, or what?"

Matt wasn't interested in what he had for breakfast. He was

absorbed in thought. "This is a line drive bat," he mumbled. "When you use it for a line drive, it delivers all of its energy to the ball in a sort of a burst. When all of the energy that the player puts into swinging the bat is harnessed..." Matt explained.

"Oh, for Pete's sake, nephew, I know what energy transfer is, it's the principle behind machines. And I'm a machinist."

"Fastball, Hotshot!" Matt called out to the mound. "Pepper; low and inside." This was Sanji's meanest pitch. Nobody hit it. Except Matt. Sanji had trouble controlling it, and Matt only called for it when they needed the strikeout. He knew exactly where Sanji's fingers would cross the laces of the ball, and where his foot would leave the ground. He knew that when Sanji tried to throw a hard fastball inside, it was an unnatural pitch for a lefty, and he would grunt as the ball left his hand.

"Ugh!" The ball was on its way. Matt watched it spin in on him, the bean-sized ball getting bigger, and lower as it closed in to the plate. It was a ball, inside and maybe low, but anybody would have swung at it. Matt leaned back and extended his arms, clubbing the ball as it entered the strike zone.

When it left the bat, Matt figured he got most of it, but he felt no sting in his fingers. The ball rocketed out between second and third at about shoulder height. Sanji spun to watch the ball crossing left-center field with the speed of a thunderbolt. His glove dropped at his feet and he instinctively ran in the direction of the ball. He had been to an air show once, in England, but he never saw anything there that moved as fast as that baseball. Costa was dumfounded. Completely.

"Nephew," he whispered to Matt, "when they sign you up for the Big Leagues, remember your old uncle, eh?"

The ball might have come to ground, but they never saw where it landed. It was well beyond the garden, in the hay field where they would never find it. "They're gonna pay you a fortune to hit like that!"

"Matt? Hey, Matt?" Costa lunged at the falling boy, but he passed out cold before his chubby uncle could get to him.

22

Pizza!

When Matt woke up, he was lying on the sofa in the living room. He could hear people talking in the kitchen. He pulled the wet washcloth off his eyes, and saw Sanji sitting in a chair, just a few feet from his head. He listened to the conversation in the kitchen.

"Maybe he's been talking to the neighbors... Maybe it's just a coincidence..."

He didn't recognize the voice.

"He was a patient of mine. Great old guy, was Jim Fox. A bit of a strange one, though. But a heck of a nice old guy. He had a younger brother, Harry. Old Weird Harry people used to call him — but he's gone. Signed his certificate of death myself." The unfamiliar voice tailed off into a mutter which Matt couldn't hear.

Sanji couldn't contain himself anymore. "Matt, you okay? You're scaring everybody."

"Shhh. Quiet." Matt waved Sanji into silence.

"He always said that he had a mission," said the voice from the kitchen, "he could have been happier if he weren't always expecting something to happen... I told him he should talk to somebody who knew about dreams, but he'd just laugh at me and tell me that 'them bearded fellers don't understand dreams'." The voice laughed quietly, "I don't know how your boy would know about him though. And that bat. I wasn't around in those days, but some

156

of the old folk around still remember the Wagner Company. You could ask Mr. Periwinkle about it. They say Ol' Jim Fox was never the same when the old codger, Wagner, died. They say Jim had a whack on the head soon after. It left him a little wonky from then on. That's what they say, anyway. I wasn't even a glint in my mother's eye when that all happened."

"Who is that?" Matt whispered to Sanji.

"It's the doctor. He's been here checking you out." Sanji looked worried. "You've been talking in your sleep! About people you don't even know!" he whispered excitedly. "Jimmy Fox, and some guy named Wagner..."

"Uh oh," Matt moaned, "What'd I say? I hope I didn't let the cat out of the bag."

"You didn't have to! Your mother is having kittens. She was going to drive you to the hospital, and I, for one, think she should have."

"I'm okay, Sanji. Just listen to what they say and play along with me." He put the cloth back on his face, and lay still on the couch.

Maria, Costa and Dr. Marconi came back into the living room. "Hasn't come around, eh, son?" Dr. Marconi nodded to Sanji.

"No, sir, not really..."

The doctor took a thermometer out of his black bag, and put it into Matt's mouth. He took a long sharp pin out of the case, and rubbed it against the bottom of Matt's bare foot. Matt's arm and leg jumped. "Well, he's responding now, anyway." Dr. Marconi took the washcloth off Matt's face and pulled his eyelid open. He put a small bright light into Matt's eye, and said, "Mmmm." And then, "Um hmmm." He turned to Sanji and frowned. "He hasn't moved? You're sure about that, are you?" The doctor doubted it.

Sanji didn't want to lie, but he didn't want to betray Matt either. "Well, not that I noticed, sir. He might have. I mean, I wasn't watching him the whole time..."

Dr. Marconi shook his head and turned to Maria. "You call me when he wakes up. I think he'll be fine, but I want to have a look at him before the day is out. Keep him warm, and call me as soon as he wakes up." The doctor had packed up his things, and was making his way out the kitchen door, when Matt whispered to Sanji.

"Psst. Yo Sanji! Is he gone? I've got it! We gotta keep them busy for a couple of hours! I know what this is all about! I've had a dream!"

"Matt, what are you talking about? You're sick, man. Don't you get it? I'm gonna call Dr. Marconi before he leaves..." Sanji was worried about Matt. First the accident, then he'd passed out last night during the ballgame, then Matt was plain nasty to him, and knocked that inside fastball out of the ballpark, and passed out again, and now he was playing games with the doctor. He didn't like this one bit.

"No!" Matt whispered as loud as he dared. "I need an hour and you've got to help me get it. Then I'll see the doctor or anybody else you like. I know what this is all about!" Sanji squinted hard at Matt, wondering if he had gone completely over the edge.

"The bat, the boy in my dream, the old man in the barn, the jackknife, EVERYTHING! It all points to the same thing!" He frowned. Then he sat up in one quick jerk. "Yes! That's it! Everything POINTS to the answer. Sanj, I'm tellin' ya. Trust me on this. We've got to get an hour free! Think, man, think. We've got to get rid of them."

"They're not going to leave us here alone, Matt! Your mom's been having fits! You should've seen her. And Costa!" He rolled his eyes. Sanji stood up and looked out at the adults talking in the driveway. "So what's with Jimmy Fox? What's all this got to do with the Boston Red Sox? When Jimmy Fox hit that homer last night, you just fell right over."

"It's not that Jimmy Fox. It's another Jimmy Fox. J.F. who owned the bat! He was waiting for me to make baseball bats - me and Costa. And my mother! Don't ask. It's too complicated!" Matt was lying down again, keeping an eye on the kitchen doorway. "You're gonna find out soon enough anyway. Trust me on this."

"You mean the guy Dr. Marconi was talking about?" Sanji was really confused. He sat down in his chair. "Well he waited a little too long. Dr. Marconi says he's dead. He died two years ago!"

"Of course he's dead!" Matt stammered, "Wagner's dead too,

but that doesn't stop him from hangin' around waiting... It all has to do with the machine, and with the bat, and with my brother."

"That's it, I'm callin' your mom." Sanji jumped up and stared at his friend. "Matt, you don't have a brother."

"I didn't mean *my* brother. I mean *his* brother."

"*Whose* brother?" Sanji was getting frustrated at all this nonsense. "You mean Fox's brother?"

"No *Wagner's* brother!"

"Who is Wagner?" Sanji threw his hands into the air. "What are you talking about? Matt, you're dreaming out loud! You're talking about people you've never even heard of!"

"Wagner," Matt whispered. "The bat, Sanji. The Wagner bat. This is all about the Wagner bat!"

"Yeah, I think somebody must've hit you with it, Matt." Sanji sat down again. "Who's Wagner?"

"He lived in the loft. He made the Wagner Whacker. The bat is the key. When I saw the bat hit the ball, I knew. Just like he said I would."

"Well I'll tell you what I think, Killburn, I think you're nuts."

"Yeah, well, I'll prove it to you. You get me an hour alone and I'll prove it to you. The answer is in the barn. In the loft. I remember. I've been up there before! On the far side..."

He started to spin again, and he fixed his eyes on Sanji. It was no good. Sanji was spinning too. He bit his lip and tried to keep himself from fainting. Suddenly, Sanji stopped spinning. He was holding one arm out, pointing to the windows. It wasn't Sanji. This was a blond boy. It was Jimmy Fox. He was calling over to somebody, calling and pointing. Matt called out to him. The boy took no notice of him; he just kept his finger in the air. Matt looked to where he was pointing. It was the middle of a bank of large, clean windows. He tried to meet the boy's eyes. He started to spin again, and he reached out, grabbing for the boy's hand.

"Matt, it's okay. It's me!" Sanji whispered. He was getting scared.

"Sanji, that's it! That is it! I've got to do this, Sanji, and you're gonna help me!"

The boys heard the back screen door bang shut, and Matt lay motionless on the couch, with the washcloth over his eyes. "One hour, Salaam!" he whispered.

"Anything, Sanji?" Maria asked, wringing her hands.

"What d'ya mean, Mrs. Zee?"

"I mean has he moved yet?" Maria looked at Sanji and thought she saw him biting his lip.

"Well, he did sort of mumble some nonsense... but I don't know what he was saying. Maybe he said 'pizza'. Yeah, he said 'pizza, I need some pizza' or something like that. I think you should go get him a pizza." Sanji was lying, and he was sure they would know it. "Last night he woke up for a pizza, right Costa?" He looked over at Costa, hoping he was dumb enough to buy the story.

"Well, yeah, Maria. Last night he woke up when I gave him some pizza..." He was dumb enough.

Maria crossed her arms and looked over at Costa. He looked back at her and shrugged his shoulders. "We could get him a pizza at the Trading Post... We'd have to rev up the oven, but it shouldn't take more than an hour or so. I got a coupla other orders to do anyway..."

"Yeah, he should be awake by then, and he's sure gonna be hungry when he wakes up! Just leave it to me, I'll make sure he doesn't do anything stupid." It was working perfectly. They were actually going to go and get him a pizza! Sanji noticed that Matt's lip was quivering. He was going to break out laughing any second. He pulled the washcloth down over Matt's face, pinching his arm hard where no one would see.

Matt groaned and Sanji put his head down near Matt's mouth, listening carefully. He groaned again, louder this time, and under his breath he said, "Get me to my mom's bedroom."

Sanji took the cue. "I think we should get him upstairs." He put his arm under Matt's head. "Come on, Costa, let's get him upstairs into bed."

Costa came around to the side of the sofa, and lifted the limp boy into his arms. Sanji led the way up the stairs.

"Where do you think you're going?" Maria said. "Dr. Marconi didn't say we should move him."

"But Mrs. Zee, he said we should keep him warm. I think we should put him in your room. It's the warmest place in the house." Sanji was halfway up the stairs, praying that this would work.

"What do you mean the warmest room in the house? It's *June* for crying out loud." She squeezed in between Costa and the handrail, and followed Sanji up to her room. They laid the boy on the bed, and Sanji put his finger to his mouth. "I think he should have complete quiet. I'll stay with him until he snaps out of it." He herded the two worried adults out into the hallway and closed the door quietly.

Matt sprang from the bed, and joined Sanji at the keyhole. Costa and Maria were at the top of the stairs. She was crying, and Costa had his chubby arm over her shoulder. "Let's go get a pizza, if he wants pizza. You can give me a hand. We'll be back in about an hour. I'll get Dr. Marconi to come back..."

"They bought it! Can you believe it? They bought it!" Matt was holding his mouth closed, trying not to laugh out loud.

"Uhh, pizza," Sanji hissed, a laugh streaming out of his nose.

"Quick. The closet!" Matt whispered.

"What are you going to do now, dress up in her clothes and slip right past her?" Sanji was beginning to lose patience with the whole crazy business.

"I told you, I had a dream. It's all in the dream. Check this out!" Matt swung the closet door open, and traced the faint outline of a small door against the back wall of the closet. "See? Now, watch this." He reached up to the shelf above the clothes rack, and pulled out a small, sharp tool, like a pointed screw driver.

"Where'd you get that?" Sanji whistled.

"I told you. I had a dream. Put a chair in front of the door!" Sanji propped a chair under the doorknob, and made sure it was well secured. Matt was fishing the point of the screwdriver into the small seam around the secret doorway. It was exactly like the spring-loaded latch in the loft. He gave the door a push, and a black hole appeared in the closet. Matt scrambled through and swung down onto a ladder. Sanji followed closely.

Down they crawled past where they knew the living room was,

and down past the basement crawlspace. Finally Matt felt the firm cold ground under his bare feet. It was pitch black. He couldn't see anything, and he only imagined the spider webs and worse that he would have to brush aside.

He felt around the cold dirt walls, groping for the passage. It was this way. The roof was high enough that he could walk slowly upright through the dank underground.

"Matt how'd you know about this place? Where does it lead?" Sanji asked.

"It comes out in the barn. I had a dream about this passageway. I knew it was here."

Sanji was muttering in the dark, keeping one hand firmly on his friend's shoulder and the other in front of his face, clearing the cobwebs from his eyes and nose.

It wasn't very far from the house to the barn, but it seemed to take forever. The ground was hard and even, but it was completely dark, and the boys moved slowly, groping for the end of the tunnel. "What are we looking for?" Sanji asked.

"I don't know. I know there's something up there, though. Everything points to it." Matt was rolling everything around in his head. When he first went up in the loft, he had seen a long rope tied to a post along the rail. He remembered wondering what the rope was for, and why somebody would tie a fat rope to the center beam of the barn. He knew now. It was for getting to the other side!

Matt thought of the boy in the loft. He must have swung over there on the rope. There was no other way over there. "You know, Sanji, if you think I'm nuts now, just wait. It's gonna get worse before it gets better. Ouch!" Matt smacked his knee into something solid. "This is it, Sanj. Up we go!" And he nearly ran up the old ladder.

The trap door was shut the same way as everything else around Butts Wagner's farm, with a snap lock from the inside. Matt had no trouble pulling back the latch in the dark, but he couldn't lift the door. "Sanji, gimme a hand with this thing... It's...really heavy."

Sanji put his back to it and between them they were able to swing the trap door and two inches of hard packed clay out of their path. Daylight swept into their dark world, and they jumped, panting, into the warm, bright barn.

"Okay, so now what, oh great explorer?" Sanji chuckled. Matt seemed so sure of himself Sanji was almost convinced he knew what he was doing. Then he heard the roar of the engine.

BAARRAAP! ZIGGAAP! HUNK HUNK HUNK BAAR-RAP! The claw arms were snapping and the rollers were rolling. Matt stood at the end of the machine with the red knob in his hand and a triumphant smile on his face.

"Couldn't have run in years, eh, Sanji? Check it out!" Matt yelled over the din of motor. He pulled the knob back in its track and the motor grunted into silence. The two boys stood looking at the still machine, not speaking. Off to the left, a small forest of toothpicks stood upright in the hard dirt floor. "I knew it would, work, Sanj. I just knew it." He was speaking more to himself than to Sanji. "Let's go."

Matt crossed over to the ladder and began climbing. Sanji stood looking up at the loft, high above him. He wasn't sure he wanted to go up there. It didn't look safe. The ladder didn't look like a picnic either. But Matt was already a third of the way up, so Sanji Salaam grabbed the bottom rung and swung himself into the climb.

Matt moved up with confidence and without fear. Sanji was not to be outdone by his crazy friend, but he kept his body tight up against the ladder, and he gripped each rung with care. Sweat was soon gathering on his forehead, and in the palms of his hands.

"Watch this rung, Sanji, it's a booby trap!" Matt called from a few feet ahead. Sanji was careful to avoid the loose dowel, and caught up with Matt's feet just as they were sliding through the trap door.

"Whoa!" Sanji gasped, "Matt, this is very cool. This is worth it. This is worth anything!"

Matt walked to the edge of the loft and smiled devilishly at Sanji. "We're not there yet."

"What do you mean we're not there yet? Where else is there to go?" Sanji looked behind the couch, into the crowd of crates and furnishings.

Matt pointed with his thumb, and smirked.

"You mean over there?" Sanji was looking across to the loft on the other side of the barn.

Matt's smile widened, and he wiggled his thumb toward the rope tied to the post. Sanji looked way up to where the rope was tied to the center beam, and then across to the far platform, and back to the broad grin on the couch. He was wagging his head slowly from side to side. "No way in the world, Matt Killburn. There is no chance I'm gonna do it."

Matt untied the rope.

Sanji was at his side in a flash, pulling on the rope to test its strength. "No way, Matt. It's crazy. You don't even know what you're after! This isn't a dream, mate. This is real. That's a *real* long way down there!"

Matt yanked on the rope and pulled himself up onto the rail. Before Sanji had time to stop him, he had pushed himself off the edge and was swinging hard across the barn. As the rope spun him around, he looked down.

He was down there. Wagner. Dressed in his ancient baseball garb, holding his lantern up into the streams of afternoon sunlight. The platform drew nearer. Matt lifted one foot from the large knot at the end of the rope, and caught the post.

He scrambled down the post and stood on the deck, breathing hard. He looked down to see the old man, but there was no one there. No man, no lantern. Sanji was calling him from the far side of the barn. "How was it, Matt? It looked amazing!" Matt stood at the edge of the deck, holding on to the rope.

"I'll swing it back over to you!" he yelled.

"It'll never make it, Matt. It's not heavy enough without anyone on it!" Sanji, panic stricken, had his hands cupped over his mouth. "If you don't throw it all the way, you'll never get back!"

"You're right," Matt called, twisting the rope around the post. "I'm going over there," he said, pointing to the large bank of windows. He suddenly remembered his dream of the pointing boy. He shook his head, rattling away the idea that he could have been the boy in the loft in his dream, and he ran to the windows.

He wiped the glass with the sleeve of his shirt, and peered out across the fields. Maybe he could see something from here. Maybe that's what he was supposed to do. He felt pretty stupid, having come all this way and now not knowing what he was supposed to do here. He put his hands on the frame of the window, and leaned his face up to the circle of clean glass. Then he saw something. Costa's truck. He was back with the pizza!

Instinctively, he ducked down out of sight of the approaching truck. As he crouched just below the window, he had the distinct feeling that he had done this before. As if he had been squatting below these windows before...

Something caught his eye.

23

The Wagner

There, just below the window sill, between the sill and the frame, was a small, smooth fold of yellowed paper. He swept it up, stabbed it into his shirt pocket, and made for the rope.

"He's here! Costa's here!" he shouted to Sanji. He grabbed the rope, paced back as far as the rope would go, and ran headlong over the edge of the deck. He looked down at the spinning barn floor. He saw the machine, the boxes of garage stuff, and the ladder, but no old man. He had a feeling he'd see the old man again. Then Sanji leaned out over the rail to grab the rope and haul him in.

"Matt, that's the coolest thing I hope I ever see! Have you gone right out of your mind?"

"Costa's back, let's move," Matt shouted, tying the rope. "Quick!" Matt was the first one down the ladder and he called to Sanji, who was fiddling with the latch on the trap door. "Leave it, Sanji, let's get out of here!"

They clambered back into the dark tunnel and this time ran the length of it. Finding the ladder up to the house was tricky. The tunnel seemed to open up into a bigger room, with more than one passage out. Fortunately, the light from the bedroom sent a dim shaft of yellow light into the pitch black, lighting their way to the top.

Matt sprang from the closet and jumped down onto the bed. Sanji moved the chair from the door, sat on it, and put the washcloth back on Matt's sweaty brow.

"Go check it out, Sanji. I'm gonna do the 'uh pizza' routine again. I could use a slice about now, anyway." He wiped his face with the cloth and watched Sanji move quietly out into the hall.

Matt pulled the piece of paper from his pocket and examined it. The card slipped out onto his chest. He picked it up carefully and looked at it. It was a very old baseball card. The picture was of a square-faced young man with "Pittsburgh" written across his shirt. At the bottom of the card, it said, "Wagner — Pittsburgh." Matt wiped his brow with the washcloth. This was a Wagner. Signed by Honus Wagner himself! Impossible...

He could hear Sanji and Maria coming along the hallway, so he slipped the card back into the paper, and into his pocket. He had the bat, the machine, the wood, and a library of information on the science of baseball, and now he had the missing piece. No wonder it would have made the old man happy! The boy would know exactly what to do with it, the old man had said.

Sanji's voice was getting nearer, talking to Costa and Maria. Matt slipped the washcloth back over his amazed face.

"I think he's coming around," Sanji chattered, "Try the pizza, it'll probably wake him up."

Maria hurried into the room, sat on the edge of the bed and put her hand against Matt's cheek. He lay perfectly still, and said nothing. She pulled a blanket up under his chin and sat with her face in her hands.

"Uhh, pizza..." he moaned.

She looked up quickly and caught him grinning. "Matt?" she said. "Are you awake?"

"Yeah... yeah," he moaned, "I think so. Is there anything to eat?" He pulled himself up on his elbows and she buried her face in his chest.

"Matt, you're all right." She was crying, and wiping his head with her hands. "How do you feel?"

"Hungry. I'm hungry. I'm fine, Mom, I'm just hungry," he said, trying to reassure her.

"Hey," Costa grinned as he swung through the door, pizza box resting on his stomach. "Welcome back to Kansas, Dorothy. How's things in Oz?"

Matt had spent many a Sunday afternoon watching the Wizard of Oz, and he knew his line: "There's no place like home, Auntie Em. I hope you didn't put anything weird on that pizza. No onions and anchovies, I hope." Sanji held up a plate, and Costa popped open the box and slid a juicy piece of steaming pizza onto it.

"Just the way you like it, nephew: double cheese, bacon, peppers and mushrooms. And a few anchovies for that 'just died' flavor." He handed Matt the plate, adding, "I'm kidding about the anchovies."

"So what about the garage sale at the Trading Post?" Matt asked abruptly, slurping up a tangle of hot cheese and steaming sauce.

"The garage sale? Hook, Matt, I'm selling the whole lot. Lock, stock and barrel! The Trading Post is a fading dream. Looks like I'm headed back out to Alberta. I've got a few skills they still need in the oil patch." Costa seemed to be talking as much to himself as to Matt. He was staring into space, not even noticing Sanji pulling a piece of the hot pie onto a plate.

"Well, what if I offered you a job right here. Machine operator. Machine operator and manager of production." Matt looked at him seriously, but with a smile.

"Maria, call Dr. Marconi." Costa cupped his hands over his mouth, "This kid is whacko!" He wagged his head, and folded his hairy arms. "What am I supposed to manage? Manager of production," he said, imitating Matt's voice. "You found oil out here on the farm?" he laughed.

"I mean it, Costa. So what about the job?" Matt was reaching for a second piece of pizza. "I'm going into business, and I can't do that and go to school, and since there's no more Trading Post, you need a job. I'm going to open up a factory right here in Fergus. I figure we need about a quarter of a million dollars to get it off the ground. No problem."

"Yeah, sure. No problem. You open a factory, and I manage it. That makes sense." Costa reached for a plate and moved the box onto the dresser, bumping Maria's combs and knick knacks out of the way. "What are we gonna make?" He was afraid that Matt was delirious.

"Baseball bats," Matt said, very matter-of-factly.

"Baseball bats. And all you need is two hundred and fifty grand? Great. That makes two of us." Costa's eyes shifted to Maria, wondering if she was thinking what he was thinking.

Matt had a big mouthful of gooey pizza. "Sho, how much do you fink a Wagner is worf if it'sh autographed by Honus Wagner himself?" Costa and Sanji stared at him blankly.

"What," he gulped the last of the hot chunk, "do you think it'd be worth?"

"A Wagner? Oh, I dunno," Costa was looking at the ceiling, one eye closed. "I've seen pictures of 'em... I dunno. Few thousand, maybe a hundred grand? What d'ya think Sanji?"

Sanji was looking at Matt, wondering what he was up to now. "Do you mean the Wagner, or the Wagner of the bat?"

"Not the guy in the barn," Matt looked at Sanji as if he were an idiot. "A Wagner. The card."

Sanji knew what a Wagner was. Anybody who knows anything about baseball cards knows what a Wagner is. "Honus Wagner, Pittsburgh? American Tobacco Company, 1909 issue?" Matt nodded, grinning.

Sanji knew more about the Wagner than most card collectors. "Well," Sanji's voice got crisper, more English, as he told it. "Gretzky and McNall bought one a few years ago for about four hundred and fifty thousand," he looked over at Maria. "Signed it's worth less, so let's say four hundred thousand dollars. Okay, I'll say four hundred thousand dollars." Sanji looked pleased with himself. Costa was nodding along with Sanji.

"Four hundred thousand dollars for a baseball card?" Maria laughed. "Are you crazy? Who would pay four hundred and fifty thousand dollars for a bubble gum card?" She was shaking her head, laughing at the two boys and the man, who should have known better.

"Well," Matt explained, "I figure that in most cases, an autograph lowers the value of a rare card, but in the case of Honus Wagner, since there are almost no autographed cards of his at all, from any year, and only a few 1909 issue, none of them autographed, then an autograph should *increase* the value of the card in this case..."

"Why are we talking about a Honus Wagner baseball card?" Costa laughed. "Let's talk about this bump on your noggin. And how you're feeling."

"Well," Matt looked sheepishly at his mother, "sort of a lot happened. But mostly, I found this." He reached into his shirt pocket and produced the card.

"What?" Costa chuckled. Sanji and Maria came in for a closer look. "What's that?" They all read the name on the card at the same time. Costa read it out loud. "Wagner — Pittsburgh."

Costa, eyes popping, looked at Maria; Sanji, figuring it was some kind of bad joke, looked at Matt. Matt looked like the cat who swallowed the canary, his mouth a thin line barely containing laughter. It was Sanji who finally spoke.

"It's a Wagner. It's *the* Wagner! It's a *Wagner*! Matt where did you get... you mean, Wagner... the Wagner of the bat? Matt, it's worth a fortune. It's..."

"We're gonna clear out the Daily Mail and Trading Post and open up the Wagner Baseball Equipment Company," Matt grinned. "Start the inventory, Sanji, we're gonna have a garage sale!" Maria swept Matt up into her arms, and he hugged her back.

"Then," he laughed over at Sanji, "we're going to one of them dream baseball camps in California! Matt Nokes, catching instructor and Ferguson Jenkins, pitching coach. We're going to the Big Time!"

Maria was hugging so hard he couldn't hold the card, and he handed it off to Costa. His uncle kissed the little card and danced it around the room before handing it to Sanji, and pulling Maria up off the bed for a waltz across the floor. Sanji marveled at the card for a minute, and propped it up on the dresser. He pulled Matt to his feet and danced him around Costa and Maria. They were all laughing and singing, "Take me out to the ball game, take me out to the crowd" when Dr. Marconi poked his head through the doorway.

"I reckon' the young fellow has recovered?" he said, looking in on the bizarre scene.

"Hey, Dr. Marconi!" Costa laughed a deep, rumbling laugh and they all stood looking at each other, and at the confused medical man. "He's up and he's beautiful!" Costa said. "He's been to Oz and he's brought back the ruby slippers from the Emerald City!"

"Toto too?" Dr. Marconi said dryly. They all broke up laughing and started into the song again. Dr. Marconi sat on the chair, scratched his head, and waited for them to explain.

24

The Hall of Fame

D r. Marconi listened to the story, and checked Matt from end to end. He couldn't see anything wrong with the boy, except for the red bump on the back of his head, and he turned his attention to the baseball card.

"I've got a friend in Cooperstown, Matt. That card belongs in the hall of fame. Let me go back to the office and make a phone call or two, and see what I can find out about it."

"Hey, I can do better than that, Doc. Here's the phone." Costa pulled the bedside telephone onto the bed and handed the receiver to Dr. Marconi.

Maria, Costa, Sanji and Matt jabbered quietly while the doctor connected to the National Baseball Hall of Fame in Cooperstown, New York. He asked for his friend, Tom Bright, and they all waited while the call was transferred. "Hi, Tom. Dominic Marconi from Canada... That's right. How are you?"

He chuckled at something the man on the other end said. "Listen, I've got a friend who has a valuable old baseball card, and I wondered if you could give me some advice..." He laughed again and shook his head. "No. Yeah, I know, *everybody* thinks they've got a valuable baseball card... Listen. I've got a Honus Wagner 1909 American Tobacco Company issue, signed by Honus Wagner."

They all waited for his response. Dr. Marconi shrugged and

pointed to the phone. "Tom? Tom? Are you there? Oh, well since you didn't say anything..."

"Yes, I'm holding it right now... Yes, it's mint... Yes, it's Honus Wagner. Is it for sale? Well of course it's for sale! That's why I'm calling you... Yes, I wanted you to have first crack at it... A thing like this belongs in a museum..." They waited a long time while the doctor nodded and grinned at his friend on the other end of the line. "Okay. Yeah, call me at," he looked at Maria and wiggled his hand. "What's the number here?"

She held up her fingers and gave him the number. "Five one nine seven three two nine nine one two...Yeah. Okay. I'll be here for an hour or so. Okay. Great, you too, Tom." He handed the receiver to Matt and shrugged his shoulders. "You've got quite a historic piece there, my boy. Tom says he's never heard of such a thing. He's going to make some calls to a wealthy company who's been looking for a suitable donation to the museum. He figures the card is worth about five hundred thousand American dollars, and McDonalds Restaurants is looking for a way to participate in the Hall of Fame. He says it's as good as sure that they'll want to buy the card and donate it to the Hall."

They all looked at each other and started laughing again.

"What are you all laughing about? This card is worth a small fortune!" Dr. Marconi looked at Maria and Costa, who were both laughing their heads off. He looked at Sanji and Matt, who were singing and giving each other high fives. "What's so funny? You're a rich man, Matt. What are you going to do with the money?"

Matt looked over at his mother, and at Costa, then he whispered something to Sanji. He grinned back at Costa and gave him a high five. "We're going to have a garage sale!"